Saga of the Selenixies
COLLAPSE OF THE CRYSTAL FORTRESS

Saga OF THE Selenixies

COLLAPSE OF THE CRYSTAL FORTRESS

KRISTIE FERRUGIARO

inspired girl
storybooks

SAGA OF THE SELENIXIES: COLLAPSE OF THE CRYSTAL FORTRESS by Kristie Ferrugiaro

Published by Inspired Girl Books, a division of Inspired Girl Enterprises
Asbury Park, NJ 07712

www.inspiredgirlenterprises.com

Inspired Girl is honored to bring forth books with heart and stories that matter. We are proud to offer this book to our readers; this book is a work of fiction by the author.

This book is written as a source of entertainment only. The author and publisher do not assume and hereby disclaim any liability in connection with the use of the information contained in this book.

Products, pictures, trademarks, and trademark names are used throughout this book to describe and inform the reader about various proprietary products that are owned by third parties. No endorsement of the information contained in this book is given by the owners of such products and trademarks, and no endorsement is implied by the inclusion of products, pictures, or trademarks in this book.

ISBN: 979-8-9878794-5-0

Editorial Director Jenn Tuma-Young
Cover Design by Alli May
Copy Editing by Janelle Leonard, Natalie Papailiou, Laura B. Ginsberg
Interior design and typesetting by Roseanna White Designs
Author Photo by Jessica Morrisy Photography

Library of Congress Control Number: 2022943716

inspired girl
storybooks

Table of Contents

This book is dedicated to those
with overactive imaginations,
those who spend their time in a daydream,
imagining a world where you can be
anything you want to be. The sky's the limit!
You have everything you need inside you,
all you need to do is let it flow.
The possibilities are endless.

I - Inspire your imagination
M - Magnify your creativity
A - Amplify the eccentric
G - Go there
I - Ignite your inner most dreams
N - Nothing is off-limits
E - Empower your vision

Note from the Author

Welcome to the Saga of the Selenixies. You are about to visit some amazing worlds to help the Selenixies navigate through seven trials in seven different lands. You will discover many interesting characters. Each one is unique and special. I hope that you see yourself in one or all of them. They are faced with many different challenges and need to use their unique skills to navigate the situation. You will see how they resolve their challenges, and you will be able to tell us how you would handle the situation.

If it doesn't make perfect sense to you, remember there is magic at play and things may not always be what they seem.

I hope you enjoy this journey and you discover more about yourself along the way.

xoxo

Kristie Ferrugiaro

*You are about to enter a different
world. The world of the Selenixies.
They live in a land called Lumina,
inside a Crystal Fortress.
Lumina was a barren land
until Goddess Selene gifted
the Crystal Fortress to Lumina.
Selene used her divine powers to make
the fortress herself, encasing handpicked
gems from her collection in each crystal.
And when the time was right, she created
the most powerful storm that ever hit
Lumina; a Selenite Storm which caused
each crystal to fully charge and explode.
Then, out of the rubble the Selenixies
emerged, each one taking on the powers
of the crystal it came from . . .*

FACT! Selene (in Greek Mythology) is Goddess of the Moon, that's why the love of the moon is called Selenophilia and those who love the moon are referred to as Selenophiles. Selenite got its name from Goddess Selene, meaning literally the stone of the moon. The name alludes to the pale reflection the stone can give.

MEET THE SELENIXIES

AURA is a natural born leader. She is very smart, headstrong, and extremely overprotective. She has a very powerful personality. She takes charge of every situation. She is the protector of the Selenixies and takes this job very seriously. She is always thinking of the best way to make their lives happier and easier. She has a kind heart but always wants to be in on the action, however, she knows when to step back and let others take the lead. Aura was encased in Amethyst.

STONE is wise, fair, and kind but totally anxious. He is always thinking of all the other Selenixies. He puts everyone else first. He is very happy and wants to see the best in everyone. He appears very confident. He is extremely athletic and often shows off his skill. He can be overly conceited at things he thinks he is the best at and thinks that he is the perfect leader for the group. However, he is always worried that dark forces could hurt his friends. He worries so much that his anxiety takes over and he overreacts. Stone was encased in Lapis Lazuli.

CHANTAL loves to love. She loves absolutely everyone and everything. And will give you unlimited chances to show your love. Chantal is the sweetest of the Selenixies and everyone seems to love her. But don't be fooled by her sweet disposition—she is one tough cookie. Chantal was encased in Rose Quartz.

ROCKY is a protector. The Selenixies look to Rocky to help them face their fears and live their best lives. Rocky is very enthusiastic and loves spending time with his friends and loves helping them. Unfortunately, he is super hyper and is always full of energy. He never fully listens before he acts. He is extremely impulsive and gets himself into some interesting situations, but always can talk himself out of the situation. Rocky was encased in Labradorite.

LEORA is always so cheery. Sunshine shines through her. She helps others raise their self-esteem. She is extremely generous. She loves to create all sorts of treasures. She sometimes can be overly positive and not realistic. She loves to see the good in everything. Her energy is infectious. Leora was encased in Citrine.

BIANCA is very soothing and calms others around her. She takes nothing seriously and thinks that the Universe will work itself out. She is very carefree and flakes on a lot of her responsibilities. She wants to just be and be in the space she is in. She has no idea how frustrating she can be to others. When others test her limits, her laid-back nature takes a back seat, and she gets extremely annoyed. Bianca was encased in Tanzanite.

LEO wants to be everyone's best friend. He instantly feels at ease when he meets new people. Leo feels he can tell them everything about himself. He is a total oversharer. He can't understand why everyone doesn't love him and feel at ease when he meets them and why they aren't insta-BFFs. He gets totally upset when others don't want to be his friend and try to avoid him and his clingy neediness. Leo was encased in Aventurine.

JETT is the antagonistic villain but has a soft side. He is an empath that feels everything, but to protect himself, he is very self-centered. He is very dark in his thinking which can be his undoing. He is very independent and can be mischievous. He can't see the other side of things and acts impulsively. He has had it with the Selenixies' way of life and is convinced that there is a better way of life outside this realm. He will do anything he can to get away from them. He has a deep love for Acacia as a friend and has a need to always protect her and do what is best for them as a duo. Jett was encased in Onyx.

ACACIA is Jett's mischievous sidekick but can spark creativity in others. She promotes spontaneity at the worst times. She can't help but stir the pot sometimes, and often laughs at others when they get themselves into sticky situations. She does, however, have a soft side. She has a weakness for some of the Selenixies and secretly wants to be friends with them. Her tough exterior masks that she is dying to be accepted and be a part of what she refers to as the "cool kids." Acacia was encased in Opal.

CASSIUS talks incessantly. He is a complete know-it-all. He is extremely intelligent and likes to make sure everyone knows how smart he is. He has too much to say about what everyone is doing and has no filter for telling them their faults. But he cannot handle it at all if the tables are turned and someone points out his flaws. He has a total meltdown like a five-year-old. Cassius was encased in Jade.

SIERRA has an energizing quality that is infectious, but she can also create chaos with the energy. She has a hard time staying on the right side. She likes to play on the dark side. She struggles with right and wrong. She tries to follow her heart, but it gets her into trouble. She is heavily influenced by Jett and Acacia and looks for their approval. Sierra was encased in Ruby.

MAGNUS has a very calm mind. He can give you a strong sense of safety with his extreme confidence. Sometimes that confidence can be misleading and cause him to do things that he normally would not do or is comfortable doing. As tough as he acts and as calm as he seems over some things, he is constantly worried about getting caught and what the consequences could be. Magnus was encased in Hematite.

ZIRA excels at helping others only see the negative side of everything. She thrives on making others unhappy. But deep down she loves all the things about Leora and wants to be her friend and craft and sing and dance. But please, that all must be keep on the DL. Zira was encased in Smoky Quartz.

THE MYSTICS

The Mystics are the overseers of the Universe.
They see everything. They were appointed by the gods
to help guide all the creatures in the Universe.
They were asked to gently guide the creatures to help
them succeed or at least not cause too much trouble.

SERAPHINA is the guardian of the Helios. She is the source of heat and power and brings confidence and courage. But, when the fire burns too much, it can express itself as anger or hatred.

CHANTARA is the guardian of the Mermaids and the Pirate Pixies. She controls the ability to flow, adapt, and bind substances as well as heal nature and nourish it.

BRISA is the guardian of Giants. She channels clear communication and self-expression. She influences the ability to act with love and compassion.

LANA is the guardian of Goblins. She is grounding and calming. She keeps the ego in balance and regulates the energy of Earth.

NEOMA is the guardian of the Selenixies. She is that from which all other elements originate, and to which they all return. It's omnipresent since it's the space between all the other elements.

THE CRYSTALS AND STONES
USED THROUGHOUT THIS BOOK

Amethyst—Intuitive, Soothing, Protective
Lapis Lazuli—Self-Expression, Wisdom, Truth
Labradorite—Instinct, Protection, Change
Rose Quartz—Unconditional Love, Forgiveness
Citrine—Happiness, Strength, Thought
Tanzanite—Intuition, Communication, Stillness
Aventurine—Luck, Opportunity, Prosperity
Onyx—Protection, Strength, Quieting
Opal—Mystical, Creative, Playful
Jade—Lucky, Happy, Health
Ruby—Passion, Strength, Courage
Hematite—Grounding, Clarity, Practicality
Smoky Quartz—Protection, Calm, Positivity
Moonstone—Intuition, Hope, Sensitivity
Goldstone—Abundance, Courage, Positive Energy
Sunstone—Joy, Empowerment, Vitality
Bloodstone—Courage, Family, Loyalty
Tiger's Eye—Self Confidence, Inner Strength, Protection
Amber—Cleansing, Renewing, Grounding

Saga of the Selenixies

BOOK I

COLLAPSE OF THE CRYSTAL FORTRESS

*With the destruction of the ancient Crystal Fortress,
the Selenixies were sent hurling through different worlds,
losing their power and connection to one another.
Dark forces are holding them back as they must complete
seven trials to recharge themselves, reunite with each other,
and regain trust in the Universe before it's too late.*

Prologue

The sun crests over the majestic mountains that protect the land of the Mystics. The sky shines with symphonic shades of pink and purple with a glowing orange ball in the center. It is the most magnificent morning Mystic Neoma has enjoyed in a long time. She stretches her arms to the air in a deep V, lifting her head to invite the sunrise to envelop her completely. Her platinum blonde hair cascades down her back like waves whispering to the wind that's gently swirling through her long locks. She takes deep breaths in through her nose and out through the mouth as she appreciates the beauty of the day that is unfolding before her. She reaches up to touch the sky, dancing her fingertips in the air.

This is the most perfect time for her daily affirmations, and with this glorious daybreak she feels her day is going to be just as spectacular. She sets her intentions for a magnificent day, blows kisses to the sky, and bows her head in thanks to the Universe.

Mystic Neoma affirms, "I am ready to take on a new day. I am full of love. Everything that is meant to be, will be. My heart is open. I attract beautiful things. I will be present in every moment. I am safe and secure. The Universe is full of endless possibilities. I am grateful for my blessings. I am at peace with the Universe."

Still reeling from her amazing morning routine, Mystic Neoma sits down with her optical lens in front of her. To the ordinary person, the optical lens looks like a crystal ball. But to the Mystics, it is the eye of the seer. They can see what is going on in other lands.

Mystic Neoma's optical lens is a glowing, perfectly round orb set on top of a sculpted base, purple in color with shimmering specs of gold. She closes her piercingly purple eyes and takes a deep breath. With her left hand, she swirls across the top of the crystal ball. The Mystics are the only ones able to harness the power of the extraordinary lens. Others have tried, but anyone who is not a Mystic sees only a clear glass sphere.

Every morning, each of the five Mystics takes her turn peering in the lens to check on her designated world. The Mystics are able to see complete visions of those worlds: the good, the bad, and the ugly. But unfortunately, the lens has its limits too. It can see the present perfectly, but the future can be cloudy because the future depends on choices that are made in the present.

Mystic Neoma recites over the lens:

> *Spin, swirl*
> *Star shine twirl*
> *Moonlight, sunrays*
> *Clear eye, bright days*

Glittery sparkles and purple stardust swirl in the lens.

Slowly, Lumina comes into focus.

Mystic Neoma smiles softly. Lumina is the land of her beloved Selenixies. She loves the Selenixies dearly. Every one of the Mystics does. The Selenixies are the most special and protected throughout the Universe.

Mystic Neoma considers herself the luckiest of all the Mystics as the guardian of the Selenixies. She enjoys peering into their world to check on them and their daily activities. Each one of the Selenixies is very special to her. Each of them has unique qualities and characteristics that make them so interesting.

And Lumina, all the creatures in all the lands in all the worlds of the Universe love Lumina: the Mystics, the Selenixies, the Mermaids, the Goblins, the Pirate Pixies, the Giants, and the Helios. Lumina is the most beautiful landscape you have ever seen. It used to be a barren land, but ever since the Goddess Selene gifted the Crystal Fortress to Lumina, flowers bloom all year round. The colors are spectacular, with the most vivid blooms of pinks, purples, and reds all dancing together. The kelly green trees reach for and unfold toward the sky, their branches endless and their brilliant leaves lush. The mountains are sharp and regal. The river runs ever so softly and stays crystal clear. Birds sing the most glorious of songs. The bees create the sweetest honey. All the woodland creatures live in the most perfect balance. Everything in this world is in perfect harmony.

Lumina is powered by an ancient power source, which is a grid of crystals. There are two of each crystal. Two Moonstones, two Sunstones, two Goldstones, two Bloodstones, and two large Selenite veins that keep everything charged. The ancient power source is part of the spectacular Crystal Fortress, which houses the most rare and beautiful crystals. The fortress is a place where all the Selenixies gather to celebrate every full moon. It is the best place in the realm to enjoy the fullness of the moon, and the Selenixies are total moon lovers.

The fortress serves many purposes. It houses the Ancient Scrolls that are filled with the history of the realm, offering the Selenixies detailed information of the past. The Scrolls discuss things that worked in the past as well as things that were disastrous. They are almost as important as the power source.

The Selenixies have lived in Lumina for their entire lives. In Lumina, there is no time. They work and play simultaneously. They emerged from the rubble as what humans would call "teenagers" and have never aged. There is no stress and aside from some personality differences, very little to worry about. They feel completely safe. They don't even realize they can leave the realm if they want to. But why would they leave? Nothing out there is as amazingly beautiful as Lumina. They spend their days picking flowers and herbs, collecting nuts and honey, and preparing for their full moon celebrations. Each has a job that complements the others, and they all work happily.

The Selenixies are completely unaware, however, that there are always others trying to get into the land of Lumina and that there are beings out there who are jealous of their beautiful existence. They want to take it for themselves. There are constant threats, but the Selenixies continue to live their best lives. The ancient crystal power source has always been so strong that it is almost impenetrable, though many have tried and failed. All of the Selenixies are living in perfect harmony in this beautiful dimension.

But today is different.

One

THE COLLAPSE

$\mathcal{S}$omething is amiss. As Lumina comes into focus, Mystic Neoma feels a pain in her heart she has never felt before. With her right hand she clutches her heart to try and soothe the pain. But it just intensifies. Her eyes fill with giant tears that roll down her cheeks.

"Sisters, sisters," Mystic Noema gently cries as she tries to stand.

Her voice is barely above a whisper. She doesn't even need to speak. Her sisters feel it, not as intensely as Neoma, but they can feel it.

They all come running.

"Neoma, Neoma," they call, as they reach out for her. They catch her just before she collapses onto the floor.

Mystic Lana's emerald green eyes widen as she peers into the lens and understands why Mystic Neoma is so distraught. The lens not only shows in real time what is happening in Lumina, it also creates an energy field where the Mystics can feel the present moment of what's happening that cannot always be seen immediately.

"Oh no, no, no, no," whispers Mystic Lana. "This is terrible. They are dancing, but there is something brewing that is very disturbing. I feel it, too, Neoma."

The sisters help Mystic Neoma back to the chair. She slowly opens her eyes to return to the lens. She has to see. She has to warn the Selenixies. But maybe, maybe it is too late. A fluster of activity illuminating through the crystal ball reveals the sheer panic on Aura's face. The Mystics gather together to look through the lens. It flashes to another scene happening in Lumina.

The Selenixies are in the middle of their favorite dance, singing joyously.

Leora is throwing flower petals in the air. Leora is the picture of sunshine; it just spills out of her. Her short curly brown hair is in pigtail puffs. Her bright yellow sundress is making her brown skin glow. She has the darkest brown eyes with long dark lashes that stretch out and curl up to her brow. Her wide smile lights up the space, as a small group of Selenixies are enjoying each other's company.

Chantal has just displayed the most amazing treats— sparkling pink and gold cupcakes and shiny taffy interspersed with the sweetest honeysuckle. Chantal is a certified girlie girl. She loves pink everything. Ruffles, tulle, and sparkles are part of her everyday outfits so it's no surprise her treats are decorated just the same. Her sweet angelic face, framed with light brown waves, is full of wonderment.

Suddenly, there is an extremely bright light. It shoots up straight from the center of the Crystal Fortress. Chantal's ocean blue eyes begin to squint.

At first, the Selenixies are in a glorious awe, admiring this beautiful light, oblivious to the destruction that is awaiting them. Next there are several explosions. They start off small but grow bigger and bigger. A tremendous boom and then another. Louder and louder. Things start disappearing. There is another boom, and then the big oak tree is gone. Another boom, and no more berry fields. The ground begins melting, disappearing. The night sky is lit up like it is the middle of the day.

Another deafening boom, and Bianca and Leo are gone. They are sucked up into the sky.

It is like nothing the Selenixies have ever experienced before. They cannot believe what they are witnessing.

It is the scariest thing Cassius and Sienna have ever seen. They grab on to each other and try not to cry.

Zira is panicked and hiding in the hollow of a tree.

Leora watches as that tree is pulled out of the ground and disappears into thin air.

Aura is trying everything in her power to stop this. She doesn't even know what this is. She has never read anything about this before. The Scrolls have failed them. She runs around frantically trying to find everyone and stop this. But no one can stop it.

Rocky and Stone try so hard to hold down the Crystal Fortress. Until the mother of all blasts comes from behind them. And then the Fortress is blown to smithereens. Crystals are raining down everywhere.

The remaining Selenixies all run together as the final blast comes from underneath them.

And then BOOM.

Nothing.

The entire world has collapsed.

Falling. Falling. Falling. The Selenixies are falling and being flung in all different directions. They try desperately to hold on to each other, but they are not strong enough. They feel like they are in a whirlwind spinning and spinning and spinning.

Then a red glittery mist envelopes them and they are whisked away.

Two

THE ASSIGNMENT

Aura opens her eyes. They are naturally hazel but change color with her mood. When she's happy, they're bright green. Other times, when fear and uncertainty take over, they are accented with thick gray bands.

"Where am I? I was just— How did I get here? And where exactly *is* here?" Aura wonders aloud. Her eyes are wide. Her long, black hair is completely disheveled, with straw and leaves tangled in her curls. Nothing feels real, everything around her is foggy.

"It can't be," she mumbles, searching the sky around her.

She looks back to see herself still sleeping on a pillow of leaves. *This must be a dream, but how? This is not making any sense.* Aura takes a minute to get her bearings, suddenly remembering the blast.

OMG no! Oh no. Her mind darts back and forth, piecing together the destruction that fell upon their beautiful land of Lumina. The blast. The source. She smooths her hair as best she can and fixes her skirt.

"How could this be? And what do we do now?" she says, looking at the unfamiliar world around her. She sits down and begins to cry, soon bawling her eyes out.

After taking a few deep breaths, she stands and wipes her face, still teary.

"Pity party, over. Now onto figuring out how I can get back to Lumina . . . if it's even still there. And where are my friends?" Aura says aloud again, even though no one is there to hear her. She sighs as she readjusts her skirt.

First, she thinks, *I need to focus on where I am.* Aura turns to explore carefully.

Holy moly, what is going on over there? There is a cauldron with herbs drying on the rack above.

All at once, she pieces together where she is, completely in awe. "This must be the world of the Mystics. How amazingly cool is this? I've always wanted to visit here." As shocked as she is from the blast, she can't help but laugh at how she's talking to herself.

"I'm so losing it," she says through a chuckle.

Aura has read all about the Mystics and this world in the Ancient Scrolls which are housed in a special scroll room in the Crystal Fortress on Lumina.

The scroll room is painted a deep purple. The gilded scrolls are kept in ornate wooden cases on the walls, each with its own special place. They are written on vellum, which looks like frosted glass; not quite crystal clear, but certainly see-through, with a smooth, almost plastic, finish. It is delicate, yet durable; strong enough to write and draw on.

In the center of the room is a hand-carved wooden

table. Here, a Selenixie can extract a scroll from the wall, lay it out, and read the history. It is open to anyone who wants to spend time there and learn. There is a special section that holds a few of the extra delicate scrolls, these are the ones with very important information. With these, you can find out about how the world came to be and how it is powered. While this room is no secret, its power could be detrimental if wielded by the wrong hands.

Aura walks down to the village and knocks on the first door she sees. The big door opens slowly, revealing a gorgeous woman with white hair wearing a flowy green dress.

"Hello, my sweet. I have been waiting for you." Her voice is like a song.

Waiting for me? This is so *weird.* But instead of fear, she feels so comfortable with the stunning Mystic. It feels natural, like she has known this woman her whole life.

As such, Aura instantly begins pouring out her heart to her about the destruction of Lumina.

Mystic Neoma gently interrupts her, as she isn't sure how long she will be able to speak to Aura through her dreams.

"Yes, Aura. I know what has happened. And it isso nice to meet you, unfortunately under these circumstances. I have heard wonderful things about you." Mystic Neoma reaches out her hand to touch Aura's face softly.

"Me?" says Aura inquisitively, surprised at this revelation. "You have heard about me. How?"

Avoiding the exact question, Mystic Neoma explains, "There are many worlds in our Universe, each unique and special. The world that you are from was the most perfect, and we are all truly saddened by the collapse."

Mystic Neoma tries to stay as calm as possible. Unbeknownst to Aura, Mystic Neoma has been watching Lumina and Aura her whole life and knows everything about her. But too much information right now might scare her off. Now, Mystic Neoma needs Aura to listen.

"I, I just don't understand. How did it happen?" Aura asks, desperate for answers. She sits down across the wooden table from the beautiful Mystic. Aura's knees are shaking below the surface and her glittery purple combat boots are digging deeply into the ground beneath her feet.

"A stone was moved," Mystic Neoma says sadly. She lowers her head, and her white hair falls into her face.

"I have read all the Scrolls, and nothing *ever* said that moving one of the stones would cause a total collapse." Aura abruptly stands, and the chair scratches across the floor.

Aura knows this, it can't be right. The Crystal Fortress is powered by an ancient power grid of crystals. Each stone in the grid works together to create a perfect balance. There were two of each; two Moonstones to help focus on inner growth and provide calmness, two Sunstones for good fortune and empowerment, two Goldstones to restore harmony and attract positive energies, and two Bloodstones to increase energy and clarity. They are all charged by a large vein of Selenite that runs underneath. Every full moon, they are bathed in the light to give them an extra boost of energy.

"You are correct, no scrolls will tell you about this.

The shield is a thin, invisible veil that encapsulates and protects the world of Lumina. It does not let anything in or out unless a grid crystal has been moved, causing the shield to lower. In this case, a Goldstone," she continues, slowly.

"There have been many who have tried to get into Lumina without permission. I traveled there myself, many moons ago. But I was invited in, the stone was moved purposefully and quickly replaced when I left," she explains, adding more context to what the scroll had told Aura before. "However, this time, the stone was moved recklessly, that is what caused the collapse. The source could feel the hate in their heart. Once there is true hate, it's hard to come back from that." Mystic Neoma moves toward Aura to calm her.

Aura shakes her head quickly, stumbling over her words. "Hate? Who would hate us? Could it have been from within? Hate within, but who? There is no hate among the Selenixies. But who else could have gotten inside Lumina?"

Images of the Selenixies pop through Aura's mind like a book as she assesses who might be the source of this feeling that destroyed beautiful Lumina and life as she knew it. The pain in her heart grows sharper as the images reveal who may be the source of this hate—two Selenixies who have distanced themselves from the group. She quickly shuts down her thoughts and turns to Mystic Neoma, who can sense her anxiety.

"So, how do we get it back?" Aura asks, very impatiently.

The beautiful Mystic looks grave. "We are all deeply saddened."

"You keep saying 'we.' Who is we?" says Aura.

"We are the Mystics, a group of five sisters that help all the creatures of the Universe live in harmony." Mystic Neoma attempts to gauge Aura's reaction.

"What do we do now?" Aura asks, she can't stay still.

"First, go find the Selenixies. All of them. You will need each other. You are more powerful as a group than you are as individuals," Mystic Neoma says firmly, trying to reassure Aura. "You will be faced with seven different challenges."

After the destruction, the Mystics were blessed with a vision from the Goddess Selene of what was to come. After much sobbing of her own, Selene knew that they needed a reason to trust each other and work together.

"Each challenge will occur in a different world, which will help you to reconnect to the Selenite's power, and you will be one step closer to returning to Lumina," Mystic Neoma explains.

The importance of the Selenixies keeping their connection to Selenite is well-known. It is the source of their good nature, their positive energy, and their overall power. Humans use food for this purpose; the Selenixies, while they enjoy food from time to time, are fueled and powered by Selenite. Aura realizes that perhaps the Selenixies responsible for the collapse have lost this connection, allowing negativity and hate to come into their hearts.

Mystic Neoma continues, "Be careful. There will be many obstacles along the way. Some will be obvious, and others may seem insignificant. They are all significant, no matter how great or small you may feel they are. Keep moving through them, charging your Selenite. Fill your heart with love and everything else will be clear."

Aura seems both overwhelmed and exhilarated by this information. She is a leader through and through, but has never had the opportunity to take charge, since the Selenixies' lives have been mostly harmonious, until now. As if a dormant need has awakened, Aura shifts her worry and fear into excitement for answering the call to the challenge. She is beginning to take this all in stride.

"Now that you are outside your protected realm, you may start to develop magical powers. Don't be afraid. On Lumina you did not need magic, but in the other worlds you may need it to protect yourselves. It's all going to be okay, just know that. I would love for you to stay with me forever. But you were meant to lead. And you are going to be amazing. Now, it's your time to show everyone what a phenomenal leader you are. Go!" Mystic Neoma knows Aura is meant for this purpose, and a push in the right direction will serve her well.

"I have so many questions." Aura starts to pace, a little frazzled. "But wait, seven worlds, and what else?"

"Lean on each other, trust each other, and work together. That is all you need to regain what you had. And just remember that it is all about balance. You will understand this as you go. When things are balanced, everything will be right." Mystic Neoma tries to give as much information as she can without pushing Aura over the edge. "Now, go. Go, lead, succeed."

"How?" asks Aura pleadingly.

"Everything will make more sense when you awaken," Mystic Neoma responds in a comforting tone.

"Okay. Here goes nothing," says Aura.

Three

THE AWAKENING

After the collapse, Stone awakens, stunned from the blast. His messy light brown hair is covering his deep brown eyes. He is dazed and doesn't know where he is. He is completely lost. He is nestled in something with a bumpy, wood texture. He can feel his limbs and wiggle his toes, but he's not sure he is ready to stand.

He discovers he is lying in is a pile of leaves and twigs. As he stretches, he hears the dead leaves crunching around him. Everything is very brown. The ground underneath his body is cold and damp, but not really wet. Nothing about this place makes sense to him. Above him is dirt, below him is dirt. To the right and left, dirt.

Where are all of my friends? What happened? Where am I? How can I get home? Where is home? Stone's thoughts are even more dizzying than the blast as searches for the Selenixies in all directions.

Stone has always been a wise, fair, and kind Selenixie but he is totally anxious. Even before the blast, he was the one Selenixie that would worry about the possibility of dark forces hurting his friends. He worries so much that his anxiety takes over and he overreacts, generally. Now that his fears seem to have been confirmed, he is in a total tailspin. But he quickly pulls himself together and focuses himself. That's the great thing about Stone, when push comes to shove, he always puts the good of others before his fears.

If I am here, then some others have to be here too, Stone thinks.

The darkness that surrounds him is unfamiliar. This is nothing like his light-filled home. He needs to get back to Lumina. And he needs to find all of his friends.

But where do I begin? Stone wonders.

He lifts himself up to begin his exploration through this unfamiliar land. It is thick with brush and dirt, bumpy roots of all shapes and sizes. As his athletic frame tries to summit each hurdle, sticks scraping his ankles all the way up to his knees, Stone regrets wearing shorts. He is trying to move as fast as he can.

"The faster I move, the faster I can figure out where I am," Stone says to the roots.

But the dirt and the roots are hindering his way. He leaps over a root, catches his foot, and falls on his face. He slams his hand into the ground, frustrated.

"This is ridiculous," Stone shouts.

He gets up, dusts himself off, and begins to climb up again through the roots. Using his strength, he swings back and forth trying to propel himself up to the next level. He hooks his legs around a large root and moves his arms to the next group of roots that is just out of his reach causing him to have to jump at it.

Thank goodness he is able to get a good grip and pull himself up to another sort of clearing. He's quickly depleting his energy level.

Exhausted both mentally and physically, within just a few minutes, he sits, broken, closing his eyes and remembering again in detail the blast, and that his beautiful, harmonious home of Lumina has been destroyed. Visions of the blast start to popcorn in his brain.

He sees everyone celebrating.

POP!

He hears a noise.

POP! POP!

He sees terror on the faces of his fellow Selenixies.

POP! POP! POP!

He sees a blast erupt from behind.

POP! POP! POP! POP! BAZAAAANGGGGGG!

He can still hear the sound of the boom and the piercing screams coming from his friends. And the smell, it was the worst thing he ever smelled. He remembers watching his friends disappear and desperately trying to hold down the Crystal Fortress.

And then nothing.

He doesn't remember anything after that. His mind is totally blank until he opened his eyes in the dirt.

What do I do now? He can't give up. *No!*

After a short break, he gets up, motivated by the thought of finding the others. As he continues to search for his friends, an intuitive thought pops in his mind that the dimension he is exploring could be Earth. But he has read some things about Earth in the Ancient Scrolls, and it doesn't resemble this dark place full of roots. He tries to remember what the Scrolls said exactly, and then his mind gathers all the information reminding him what the Scrolls said.

Earth is described as a world that was similar to Lumina. Similar in plants and animals but not as beautiful. It is inhabited by humans. Humans seem to be similar to the Selenixies in some ways. Two arms, two legs, walking upright. Two eyes, a nose, a mouth, two ears, each one unique in their own ways. But their demeanor is different. According to the Scrolls, humans on Earth can be shorter tempered, treat each other poorly, and just don't get along as peacefully as the Selenixies do on Lumina. Humans are born as babies, and they age to be almost one-hundred years old. Some even older. The Selenixies have no concept of time or aging.

The Scrolls describe layers of rock that created the earth. One of the layers is made up of molten rock—this is the crust that makes up the surface of the earth as well as the underground. The Scrolls explain that many of the inhabitants live on the surface but there is a whole other world that lives underground beneath the surface. The Scrolls explain that everything living is rooted in the soil and goes beneath the ground. It says that the roots and the soil were the support system of the land.

"Oh," Stone says, a bit scared when realizing the roots must be underneath the trees of Earth he has read about in the Ancient Scrolls. "This isn't good."

Stone was definitely underground. He could not see the sun, the moon, or the stars. The underground was like a series of obstacles, kind of like the obstacle courses that Rocky loved to set up for them to race through. The roots are everywhere. The roots are so thick and coarse. In every direction they twist to the left and to the right.

"I must be underground," says Stone.

It is so very dark. He begins searching for more light. *Maybe if I climb up I can get to the surface.* So up he climbs. In some areas the roots are so thick that it is extremely hard to maneuver. He barely fits through some holes. In other areas it is easy, almost like a set of stairs leading to the next level closer to the surface. The climb is tedious and hard. It is taking a lot of effort, especially not knowing if he is going the right way.

Finally, he comes to what looks like the surface. The roots have thinned a little and there is a clearing. He needs to regroup and come up with a plan.

Four

TRIAL 1 PART 1: EARTH

Across the way, nestled in a large dip of root, Aura begins to wake up. She opens her eyes and sees she is in a strange, dark place. She remembers her conversation with Mystic Neoma and thinks perhaps her time in the land of the Mystics was all a dream. But to the Selenixies, dreams all have messages within them. *If that was a dream, what does it mean?*

Suddenly, a deep knowing overtakes her, and she realizes it was more real than a dream. She must trust her instincts. She must trust the Mystics and the Universe, and everything will be okay. She looks around, becoming strangely aware of all the thick roots that have created a maze. She remembers the trials Mystic Neoma told her about and knows in her heart this is the first of seven.

"Focus, Aura," she says out loud. "Just feel."

Mystic Neoma told Aura that before she begins the trials, she needs to find her friends. Finding the Selenixies becomes her first priority. She stands on top of the root and balances herself as if on a balance beam. She stretches both of her arms out wide and walks the roots up and down on the hard, dusty surface. As if she is sanding the surface with her sharp steps, bark scrapes off creating a cloud around her.

Ewwww, what is this stuff? Aura thinks.

Lumina has lush green grass and colorful flowers of every variety. This land is the total opposite, and the dust is making her feel a tickle in her throat. She begins to get nervous, and balancing becomes more of a challenge. She decides to shift her thoughts to peace and friendship, navigating through the mess of roots with ease.

As soon as she is feeling confident in her ability to walk on this maze of roots, she sees a familiar friend. Stone sits on roots up ahead. *Of course, it's Stone.* In Lumina, wherever Aura is, Stone isn't far behind. She has a great friendship with Stone. It doesn't surprise her at all that she has found him first. She doesn't want to startle him, so she lightly calls his name.

"Stone," she says as she carefully navigates around the roots toward him.

He isn't sure exactly what he hears, but he turns and sees Aura coming toward him. He is so relieved to have a friend. *How awesome, a friend!* Stone thinks. He is so happy to see Aura that he runs toward her, balancing himself on the roots without a thought.

They hug and feel such peace in that hug. It is a long hug. Aura takes a deep breath and releases it, melting deeper into Stone's arms.

They have so much to talk about, and they will talk about everything at some point in time, but right now they just need to bathe in each other's light. Things are starting to look up.

"Oh, Stone, I am so happy to see you. I was so frightened after the collapse," she says. Even as she talks about the collapse, Aura's calm starts to transform into absolute distress.

"Who would have thought that was going to happen? I have never read of anything like that happening anywhere in the Ancient Scrolls," Stone says. He is disappointed in himself. He starts to take this burden on himself, like he has some fault in it.

"Me either," says Aura. "But wait, I have to tell you I had the most intense dream. It was more like a vision. I was in the Land of the Mystics, and I spoke to the most beautiful Mystic, Neoma. She explained it all to me. We would have never found it in the Scrolls because we have never had hate in our hearts."

Aura is always very animated and speaks with her whole body, especially her hands.

"Hate? How could hate have caused the collapse? Who hates us? Who would want to collapse our Crystal Fortress? What purpose does that solve?" Stone asks.

"This was done from the inside. One of us, one of the Selenixies has hate in their heart. I think it has to do with not having enough Selenite. I haven't figured it all out yet. But if one of us is feeling hate, we have to surround everyone with love to counter it. And we need to keep our Selenite charged."

Stone stands very still. He is normally not a crier, but giant tears form in his eyes.

Aura tries to calm him down.

"I didn't believe it either. With a heart of love and light, you can move a gem so that outsiders can enter or exit," Aura says, wanting to fill him in on all of the information from Mystic Neoma.

"I read that too," answers Stone. "But it didn't say anything about love and hate."

"It wouldn't," says Aura. "There has never been anyone who had hate in their heart." Aura can sense his level of anxiety rising quickly.

"OMG, WHO IS IT?" screams Stone. Aura knows he isn't yelling at her; he is just yelling in total frustration.

"I don't know." Frustrated herself, Aura knows they need each other to figure this all out.

"But I am having a hard time thinking who it might be. I know some of us are closer than others, but hate? It just doesn't seem possible. I'm scared," Stone says.

"Me too," Aura says. "Me too!"

They hug each other again, trying to comfort one another. It helps a little.

She continues to tell him all the things Mystic Neoma told her. "Neoma is the Mystic assigned to help us. She told me that we would be faced with seven different tests, and each one would force us to work together to get to the next step."

"Okay," says Stone, who is always up for a challenge. "If we complete all of these challenges and recharge our Selenite, can we return home?"

"That's what she said," answers Aura.

"Did she give you any idea of what the challenges might be?"

"No, but she told me that we have to find our friends," adds Aura as they start to walk again and explore the area around them.

Stone really wants to meet Mystic Neoma, and Aura promises that one day they will, but first they have a lot of work ahead of them.

She realizes she forgot to tell him something. "Stone, we have magic."

"What do you mean?" Stone is confused, but he can see Aura's excitement. And this sounds like it is good news.

"Back on Lumina, we didn't need magical powers, so they laid dormant. But now that we are in danger, they will come to the surface. I don't know exactly what the magical powers are, but they will continue to emerge as long as we are in danger." Aura hopes like heck Stone doesn't think she's out of her mind.

She goes back into confident, leader mode. "It's going to take a lot of perseverance and teamwork."

"You know how I love teamwork," says Stone, trying to look on the bright side.

It is getting late, and the pair is exhausted from the events of the day. They find a safe spot in the tree root and sleep soundly for the first time since the blast.

When the two rise from their slumber, there is a very angry Jett standing over them.

Jett resembles a bit of a pirate with spiky hair, thick beard with beads within it, and a mustache covering his upper lip. His clothing is black like his mood. With his rough exterior, Jett also has a soft side.

He is one of the Selenixies that Aura and Stone aren't the closest with, but they are happy to see him nonetheless, and tears fill both their eyes.

Jett is an empath but does his best to cover it up. He

turns his head to hide his own watering eyes, squints, and turns back to the pair.

"Ugh, can you two stop feeling? It is too much for me," Jett says, jumping down to the clearing below.

"Great, doesn't everyone want to wake up to a grumpy Jett?" grouses Stone.

"Jett, I know you are a big softie under all that grumpiness," teases Aura.

The pair giggles, and Jett just shrugs and smirks. Jett feels a little bad that Aura and Stone give him so much credit. He was questioning if he was a big softie or a sinister snake that fooled everyone.

"Where did you come from?" asks Stone.

"Really, do you care? I don't. I only care about how you two goody-goodys are going to get me out of here and help me find Acacia," he demands.

"Great way to start the day," says Aura.

Aura fills Jett in on her dream and all the information she has. Jett just doesn't seem to care, and this saddens Aura. She tries not to take any of this personally because she knows they have to work together. She knows he has a heart and begins to wonder if he may be low on Selenite himself.

"Let's just get to work," barks Jett.

"We are clearly beneath the earth in roots, and roots normally grow upward, so maybe we should continue to climb up so we can get out of here," Stone says.

"Earth! Roots! Yes!" says Aura excitedly as if they finally cracked the first code. She continues a bit more calmly taking on the tone of a leader. "Good plan, Stone. That makes sense."

"This is not going to work," Jett grumbles, not convinced, as he begins to climb behind Stone.

"Why is it not going to work?" asks Stone.

"We have to make this work," Aura says.

The arguing continues as the trio climbs up to the next clearing.

"What's the use? There are just more roots," adds Jett, already done with this situation.

"Mystic Neoma said that if we don't work together, we will never be able to leave this world," states Aura. "So, let's come up with a plan we can all agree on—a plan that makes us all feel comfortable—and then let's execute that plan." If Jett is invested in the plan maybe he won't complain so much.

"Make us comfortable? Aura, are you kidding me? This is not comfortable. Comfortable would be Acacia and me in a hammock by the old oak tree. Far away from all the drama. This is not comfortable," yells Jett.

"We get it, this is not ideal for us either. You think we want to be here? Let's just make a different plan. What do you want to do?" asks Stone. "We all need to be on the same page. And everyone will have a say in our movements." Stone knows that if Jett doesn't have a say in the plan he will never participate in it.

"I think we continue to climb up, and maybe we will hit the surface, since we are in the roots, ya know," says Jett.

"Great plan, climb up," says Stone being supportive.

Five

TRIAL 1 PART 2:
ROCKY AND THE SPIDER

Still unconscious from the powerful blast, Rocky is in a dreamlike state. He is in the fight of his life, though. Hit them with the left and then a right, uppercut. Right hook! He is throwing punches in all directions.

"How come I can't use my arms?" mumbles Rocky. "What is going on?"

He is completely bewildered.

Rocky hasn't opened his eyes yet, but he is fighting with all his might. *This must be a dream. Wake up*, he yells to himself. *Wake up! Fight, fight you must fight this!*

"You have trained for this your whole life, FIGHT!" he says aloud, but his voice is barely audible. "But who am I fighting?"

Rocky loves to be physical and fills his day with activities that help keep him in extremely great shape. He loves to run and do anything that involves working out. He is always ready for a fight even if it is normally just messing around. But now when it really counts, and he feels like he needs to protect himself, he can't move his arms.

I have to fight this, but I need to wake up.

He is willing himself awake.

With a huge gasp he roars to life. His eyes snap open. And he lets out a huge bellowing scream. The sound echoes through the cavernous roots. His eyes are wide, searching and searching for something, even though he is not a hundred percent sure what he should be looking for.

"Wait, what is this?" he yells. He is trying fiercely to move his extremities.

Rocky is looking up and down his body.

His arms are pinned to his side and his legs feel like they are bonded together. He is wrapped from neck to toe with white string. He begins to struggle. He knows there has to be a way to get out of this. *No one ties Rocky up!* he thinks.

The more he struggles the tighter the string gets. Panting from all the fighting, he exhales loudly. *Okay, okay, think this through, Rocky.*

"The more I struggle, the tighter it gets, so relax," he states out loud. "There must be a way out, I just need to use my brain instead of my brawn."

He then smiles and chuckles at the joke he made.

And here she comes. Ever so slowly down her web.

Her movements are simply elegant. All eight legs work in unison. It makes her stalking look like a well-choreographed dance.

As for her web, she has been working on this for years. It is absolutely stunning. The patterns are so intricate. Each silk is perfectly placed. She spends all her spare time, which is the time she is not eating or sleeping, spinning her silk. It is truly a magnificent sight. She creeps down the web humming as she always does as she heads to her next meal. And boy is she hungry today.

She caught something late yesterday but was way too tired to eat the whole meal. She hates to waste food. So, she simply wrapped him up for safe keeping.

It was time now and she is dreaming of how yummy it will be.

She inches toward him. He is awake. *Oh, what fun this will be*, she thinks.

Rocky catches a glimpse of her and starts to struggle again. He is not going out like this. Even though he isn't sure what this is.

Rocky yells over to her.

"Yo, umm. You there. Hi, I'm Rocky. There must be a mistake. Can you help me get out of this?"

She shakes her head and smiles all the time moving closer.

"What exactly is happening here?" he questions out loud to himself.

"I am a spider and you my dear are my dinner," says Ally licking her lips.

"There has been a mix-up, I am not anybody's dinner," Rocky replies, surprised the spider can speak and is actually having a conversation with him.

"Oh, but my sweet you are, and you are going to be delicious." Ally moves in just a little closer.

"Listen, you don't want to eat me. I would be gross, very gamey, ya know. You would much prefer a fly or a bug or something." Rocky is doing anything to distract her.

"No, you will do," Ally answers.

"Wait, you can't eat me. I am a Selenixie," he exclaims.

"What? You're a Selenixie?" asks Ally. "I have heard about the Selenixies but never had the chance to actually meet one."

"So, you'll let me out of here then?"

"I didn't say that," replies Ally. "I wonder how good you will taste." She edges a bit closer.

She sees the fear in Rocky's eyes, and this makes her giggle. She reaches in like she is going for it.

Rocky lets out a huge scream, "NOOOOO!"

Ally is a bit of a prankster like Rocky. She reaches over and cuts the silk to free him.

"Stop, you big baby. I am not going to eat you. Relax."

She is a tiny bit disappointed and still terribly hungry.

The moment he said he was a Selenixie, she knew she could no longer eat him.

"So, why are you down here?" she asks.

"Not really sure," responds Rocky. "We were getting ready for our celebration and then boom, some crazy blast happened and the next thing you know, I am stuck in your web. Weird right?"

"It is peculiar that you would end up inside the earth and not on top," says Ally.

"Nothing really makes any sense at all," states Rocky. "But wait, where is everyone else?"

"Are there others?" she asks.

"Yeah, like all my friends. Do you think they are stuck

down here too." Rocky looks hopeful for the first time since he opened eyes.

"Hop on, we can go look, I know my way around." Ally says with a smile.

"You don't have to ask me twice." He jumps on her back and off they go in search of the others. A new friendship is formed as Rocky and Ally share stories and talk about their lives while Ally takes Rocky on an incredible journey through the bottom of the earth. Rocky is just a little worried because he is not sure where the others are.

Six

TRIAL 1 PART 3:
LET THE REUNIONS BEGIN

As the other Selenixies continue to climb through the roots, they hear a familiar voice.

"Yooooo, Stone, what is up, dude? Took you guys long enough to get here. I mean, I have been waiting a long time for you guys, and I am starving," bellows Rocky.

Rocky is Stone's bestie, and he is so excited to see him that he nearly jumps in his arms. They hug roughly, patting each other on the back. Rocky is the type of guy that everyone loves to be around. He sports a super short, buzz cut. His bright green eyes dazzle with excitement, even in this less than stellar situation.

"Hey, Aura, I see you, girl. Where is my hug?" asks Rocky, a giant, contagious smile lighting up his whole face.

Aura welcomes one of his giant bear hugs. She is so happy to see him. They will need his help if they are ever going to get out of here.

Sill holding Aura in his massive arms, Rocky sees Jett standing there with his normal twisted look on his face.

"Holy moly, dude, Jett, my main man, you're here too! This is awesome," says Rocky in his booming voice. "You didn't tell me Jett was here too," speaking to the giant spider behind him.

Aura doesn't see the spider at first, but when she finally sees it, she starts stammering. "Umm, OMG, spider!" yells Aura.

This wasn't just any spider. At nearly three feet tall, Ally is almost as tall as Aura and is twice as wide. She has a dark gray fuzzy body with big, round eyes.

"Chillax, she is my buddy. Her name is Ally," says Rocky.

"But she looks like she could eat us," Aura says.

Rocky smiles again, knowing his spider friend would never hurt them. "She could, but she won't. She is really chill, and she told me all about you guys being down here. But she couldn't reach you. We had to wait till you climbed up to this level," adds Rocky, all proud of his new buddy.

"How did you find her?" asks Stone.

"After that crazy blast, I ended up on her web. You have to check it out. It's absolutely stunning," Rocky continues.

"I thought she might wanna eat me, but you know me; I talked my way out of it, and now we are best buds. She said that once you guys got here, she would show us the way to the surface," he goes on.

"I wanna see her web," Aura says.

"Absolutely! Follow me," answers Rocky.

They follow Ally and Rocky to her web. It is as magnificent as Rocky says it is.

The pure white silk glitters against the dark red roots. Each string is strung in the most beautiful symmetrical pattern. It is easy to see that she has spent many days working on it. It almost looks like a cloud.

"Can I touch it?" asks Aura.

Ally gently nods.

"Yeah, but be gentle," says Rocky.

"Of course," adds Aura. "It's kind of sticky."

"Yup, that's how she traps her dinner."

"It's amazing," Stone says.

"It is," agrees Rocky. "Spiderwebs are just like life. We are constantly weaving our story, just like she weaves her web."

"Huh, I never thought of it like that," says Stone.

"Beautifully said," adds Aura.

"Great." On the outside Jett's playing it cool, but on the inside he relates to the words Rocky spoke about life. Quickly pushing his feelings aside, Jett continues, "Now can we get out of here? I am starting to get really tired."

"Yeah, no problem," says Rocky. "Ally, can you lead us out?"

The spider nods again, motioning for them to get on her back. Hesitant at first, they all climb on. Each Selenixie straddles their legs around the spider as if she is a horse. Ally moves very quickly through the roots. You would think that the ride would be bumpy and rough, but it is super smooth. She is careful with her passengers as she climbs upward. She slowly carries them up through all the roots to just below the surface. They are able to hold on to the hairs that cover her back. She lowers one of her back legs so that they can use it as a step stool. She comes to a stop right before they breach the surface. Ally lowers her hind legs again so that the Selenixies can climb down.

They hop off Ally's back one by one.

Aura is keeping high alert for the other Selenixies, with Stone doing the same.

Rocky is just as bubbly as ever, excited to be on this crazy adventure and grateful to his new spider friend.

Jett is sleepy and slowly stumbles off Ally's back, nodding at the spider in thanks, and continuing a bit behind the others.

Ally retreats the other way through the roots weeping a little. Ally never liked goodbyes, but this one was especially hard because Rocky was the first friend she'd made in a while who wasn't frightened of her at first.

"Ally says the surface is just through there," Rocky says pointing to a hole just a few feet away. The hole is small, but hopeful with a little light peeking through.

They walk a few steps toward the hole and are sizing up how they can lean in and squeeze through it to reach the surface of Earth. There are still bumps so the walk is slow and measured. There is a problem, though. Jett is not walking with them. Aura, Stone, and Rocky turn to see Jett out cold on a root. Rocky walks back but can't seem to wake him. The day must have just gotten to Jett, and fatigue must have set in.

Jett is peaceful when he sleeps, and all the roughness seems to melt away.

Rocky looks at Stone and Aura with a knowing wink,

and one by one they find a spot to nestle in. They are all a little tired, and it is getting late, so they decide to breach the surface after some sleep.

Seven

TRIAL 1 PART 4:
SUNFLOWERS AND
THE SURFACE

Jett's peaceful rest is broken when he wakes up in a panic.

"OMG, what just happened? What did I do? Where is Acacia? I hope she is not hurt. What did we do? This can't be happening! I need to find Acacia, and then everything will be okay. It wasn't us. I mean it was, but it wasn't because we didn't think. We didn't want this. I can't believe I rode a spider. I didn't mean. The grid. The destruction. I am not saying anything . . . I just need to find Acacia." Jett is rambling, and most of his words are incoherent.

Acacia and Jett have been besties for as long as anyone can remember. Acacia is the ying to Jett's yang. They are inseparable. He wants to find her and fast. Thank goodness Jett and Acacia's bond is so strong.

OMG, I am still in these crazy roots, Jett thinks as he stands.

He frantically shakes Aura, Stone, and Rocky to wake them up, hoping they will help him find Acacia.

Wait, I just need to be still. His connection with Acacia is so strong he can feel her if he just clears his mind and focuses on her. So, he sits on a rock and crosses his legs, places his hands in his lap, and closes his eyes. He begins breathing deep, cleansing breaths and thinks only of Acacia.

Breathe in. Breathe out. Breathe in. Breathe out.

He is starting to sense her.

Breathe in. Breathe out.

He can feel her. She is close to him, not far at all. She is in a beautiful place. But where? And how does he get there?

Breathe in. Breathe out.

I think I got it now. Jett feels calm now that he knows Acacia is safe. And he thinks he can find her. The connection is so real that he knows Acacia can feel it too.

Then Jett sees Acacia in his mind's eye. It feels different, like a superpower Jett didn't have before. They have always had a deep connecion and could feel each other's presence. But being able to see Acacia in real time in his mind even though she wasn't within his visual range in actuality? Totally new.

The vision comes into focus. He sees Acacia smiling. Her bright blue eyes are twinkling. Acacia knows Jett will find her. And all will be okay. He is happy that she seems to like the place she is in. It is rather beautiful, and she is free to just be Acacia. Even though Acacia has a hippie vibe, she hasn't been much of a free spirit. She has been holding a lot of pain and jealousy toward the other Selenixies.

Of course, she doesn't say that out loud and Jett dares not mention it either. But their bond is beyond words, and he knows for all her aggravation and sinister smiles, there is a pure heart that feels hurt, left out, and lonely. Now, although alone, she is wildly happy.

She is in a big field filled with sunflowers. The sunflowers are giant, so she is able to hide easily. She just wants to melt into this field and soak in the sun. She has no interest in being found. Well, aside from Jett. She misses him terribly, and they have never been apart from each other, so it is kind of weird to be alone.

When he tries to sense her, she feels it and is able to show him where she is. She doesn't know how he is going to get to her, but she knows he will find her. They are meant to be together.

But, for now, Jett can see Acacia is enjoying her time among the sunflowers. He closes his eyes again and is snapped back to the moment where he is, just below the surface.

Now that the others are awake, Jett has to get above ground. Extra motivated by his recent superpower vision, this is urgent. His shaking of Aura, Stone, and Rocky becomes faster and more crazed.

"Okay, okay," says Rocky knowing how important it is to Jett. "Let's go. We'll find Acacia."

Aura and Stone are ready too, and the four of them all flow through the hole to the surface. They think that this will portal them to the next challenge, but it doesn't. They end up in a giant sunflower patch.

Jett's face lights up. He knows this place. Jett flits up to the top of a tree and focuses his thoughts on only Acacia. Another superpower revealed.

Flitting never happened on Lumina. Flitting is like flying, just not as smooth. The Selenixies don't have any wings or way to flit on Lumina, but it seems here they have the ability to transport themselves this way if they want to get somewhere quickly. And when they do, holographic wings appear.

Just feel, Jett. Be present in the moment and feel. He is going to find her. It is non-negotiable.

"Acacia, Acacia! Feel. Feel. Got it! I have to go." Jett takes off flitting faster than before to find his bestie Acacia.

Aura, Stone, and Rocky are amazed at what they see. Jett's wings are extraordinary. They have an urge to flit too. They somehow know they can if they just close their eyes and visualize it. Mystic Neoma was right—their superpowers are being revealed. Aura, Stone, and Rocky activate their wings and flit as fast as they can, but Jett is on a mission and flitting faster than he ever thought possible. They struggle to keep up, and so they take in the beauty of the earth around them as they have freedom to do so.

Wow. Sunflowers for as far as I can see, Aura thinks. *Just incredible!*

Acacia is among the sunflowers, but Jett hasn't been able to zone in on her. Now Jett is off searching desperately.

I need to find her now! NOW! His faith in the Universe is failing. He needs her.

"Acacia! ACACIA! ACCCCAACIA!!" He screams over and over again. It is almost a cry. "ACACIA!"

And then . . . she appears! And it is like he is seeing an angel. The most amazingly perfect angel. Although, angel may be a bit of a stretch considering she has a bit of a mischievous side to her.

Back on Lumina, Jett and Acacia bonded over plotting to leave the group. Acacia would make snide remarks calling Aura and the others "fake" and wondering if aside from Jett any of the Selenixies were their true selves.

But here on Earth, it seems her sinister side is fading away and her angelic side is emerging. It is like she is glowing. She has the biggest smile on her face. She is so relieved to see Jett too. And then Aura, Stone, and Rocky at his side.

Acacia thinks, *I wonder why Aura seems happy to see me? I will ask Jett about that later.*

She is so relieved to see Jett. And she has so much to tell him. At no time at all has she ever doubted him. She knew he would find her because of the most perfect visual clues she sent him. She can't wait to get Jett alone, but Aura, Stone, and Rocky want to chat and find out all the details. She gives them the short version.

Blah, blah, blah, collapse. Blah, blah, blah, hurrying through portals.

The same story she is sure they all know and experienced themselves, except she was above the surface while they were below.

Landed in a sunflower . . . Met a cool hummingbird that showed her the best flowers and where she could hide, and that's what she did . . . Hid because she thought nobody cared to see her . . . End of boring story.

There are some more juicy details, but those are only for Jett.

Acacia and Jett drift down to the ground.

"What do they know? And what the heck happened? Jett, I wanted to leave, but I didn't want all this. You know that, right? I thought we covered all the bases. Just move one stone. It was supposed to be easy peasy to open the shield and leave. We must have moved the wrong crystal. I know I studied the Ancient Scrolls, and I know I moved the right one. But who knows. But the good thing is we are now free to do whatever we want," Acacia says in one giant breath.

You see, before the collapse, Acacia and Jett had been spending time reading the Ancient Scrolls. They felt that Aura and Stone should not be the only ones who knew it all. They felt they needed to have all the information as well. However, they thought that Aura and Stone would be totally against this because it was only for their knowledge. But that was totally untrue. They would have loved to share the Scrolls. The information was there for all the Selenixies to read. So, they would sneak around and sometimes only read small parts of the Scrolls.

Then on that dreaded afternoon while everyone was preparing for the full moon celebration, they slipped into the scroll room and found the Scroll that talked about lowering the shield. They were excited at the possibility of leaving Lumina.

Well, technically, they didn't want to leave Lumina, they just wanted to take a trip, a break from Lumina.

They wanted to see what was beyond the shield. What if there were others like them outside of Lumina? Maybe there were others that they fit in with better.

Jett explains the situation and Aura's visit from Mystic Neoma. "Acacia, do you think we have hate in our hearts? Is that even possible? I know we drifted from the others. I know we wanted out of Lumina. Hate seems extreme and I do believe that you didn't want to destroy Lumina. Mystic Neoma probably knows it was us, she's just testing us." Jett's softer side is coming through as he lowers his head in shame at what's happened to their home.

"Of course, we didn't mean to destroy Lumina," Acacia says trying to convince not only Jett but also herself that this whole mess is not their fault.

"You're right." Jett continues to tell Acacia that they need to get through seven challenges, recharge their Selenite, and then they can be free. If they don't get through them, they will be stuck here.

Acacia agrees to put their plans on hold for the time being.

Aura, Rocky, and Stone try to see if there is a portal or something that may help them get out of here. Hoping that finding Acacia is their final challenge in this world, they try to flit upward hoping that the sky will portal them to the next world and the next set of obstacles.

Aura comes to an abrupt halt. Something is off. Well, not off in a bad way. She just has an overwhelming feeling of happiness and sunshine. Maybe it is just the sunshine. But no, it is a feeling.

"It must be . . ." says Aura, confused. "No, wait. It

can't be. I can feel them, but who is it?" She flits around in a mini circle.

"Please stop. You are making me dizzy," says Rocky playfully.

"Okay, Aura, stop and just feel," she repeats to herself. Aura lands on the edge of a beautiful nest to try and focus. She turns to see three tiny baby birds in the nest.

"Okay, Aura, focus," she repeats. "FOCUS!"

Rocky and Stone land on the ground at the base of the tree next to Jett and Acacia to wait for Aura.

"What is going on?" Acacia asks.

"Aura needs a minute. I think she is on to something," says Stone.

"I hope she is focusing," mocks Jett.

"Give it a rest," barks Stone.

Rocky laughs one of his big belly laughs. "Jett is good at that."

Jett shoots Rocky a menacing glare.

Rocky isn't fazed. To him, Jett is not scary at all.

Aura is having a hard time getting in the zone with the babies chirping. So, she decides to go into the nest and play with the babies for a second. Then she can get back to the task at hand. As she jumps down, to her surprise, out steps Leora, with sunshine shining through her. No wonder Aura is feeling so cheery and bright. Of course. Leora has always made her smile. As a matter of fact, Leora makes everyone smile. Aura is so excited to see her that she leaps into Leora's arms.

"Oh, Aura! I am so happy you found me. I didn't know what to do or where I was. What happened?" questions Leora.

"I am not sure," Aura answers. "I am trying to find as many of us as I can so we can all be safe until we figure all of this out. How did you end up here?"

"I woke up to the baby birds snuggling me, and it made me feel calm. I felt like I was keeping them company when their parents were out searching for food. I felt safe hiding in their feathers. I just knew that if I stayed still that someone would find me. I don't mind much hanging out with the babies. They are sweet and love to cuddle. They brighten my day with their sweet songs."

Aura is happy that the birds helped Leora during this difficult time. But now it is time to return to Stone, Acacia, Jett, and Rocky.

The Selenixies are coming together one by one!

"How do we get down to the ground?" Leora asks as she peers over the edge of the nest.

Aura smiles and her wings unfold behind her. Leora's eyes light up at the beautiful holographic wings before her. Before she can even ask, her own wings open for the first time.

"We flit," says Aura, winking as she takes Leora by the hand. Together, they leave the nest and flit to the ground to meet the others.

Everyone is so excited to see Leora as they gently hover over the ground.

Aura hears Mystic Neoma's voice in her head telling her that she is doing a great job. She looks up to the sky and blows a single kiss in acknowledgment. When she opens her hand back up there is a Tiger's Eye in it. She places it in her pocket and begins to relax a little.

As soon as everyone's feet are grounded, an orange cloud of glitter appears.

They all say in unison, "I am strong, steady, and grounded."

The orange stardust swirls faster as the portal opens. It spins around them, enveloping them within the cloud of orange glitter. Their Selenite is recharging.

They feel light as they're whisked away in a spiraling tunnel.

Eight

TRIAL 2: ISLA OCEANIC

It is now sunset, and the sun is glowing, creating an intense orange vertical layer cake that is kissing the crystal blue ocean. The sky is lined with exquisite layers of tangerine, pumpkin, carrot, and papaya slices. It is an amazing sight to behold.

There is a certain serenity as the whole group looks out on the horizon. A peace that they recognize was last felt in their perfect world of Lumina. With hearts heavy with memories, they start to hatch a plan to get back there.

"Once we found Leora and all stood together, we were portaled here," says Aura, trying to wrap her head around how this is all working.

"There must be some of our friends here. Finding them is the obstacle that the Mystics must have been talking about, right?" Stone scratches his head, looking confused.

"Do we have to look for others?" asks Jett. "You all are already too much for me." Jett folds his arms over his chest and plops down in the sand.

"Jett, I know that this is a lot for you, but we all want to get through this, so we just have to act fast. There are Selenixies out there who are scared and alone, and it is our job to reunite them," Acacia states, trying to reason with him. Her bright blue eyes twinkle with a hint of her sinister behaviors. With short brown hair and a hippy vibe, Acacia's look is a juxtaposition to Jett's. She appears much more laid-back and innocent than she is.

"Yeah! Don't care. Nice try though!" Jett snarks.

"We have to find the others." Stone steps into the middle of the group, trying to focus on the task at hand and turning his back to a pouting Jett.

Aura, next to Leora, is distracted at the moment, which gives Stone the perfect opportunity to jump in and lead.

"Let's put our heads together and create a strategy to cover this world. It looks like an island, and we will have to see who is out there," Stone continues, at his best when he is in charge.

From the land where they are standing, water is surrounding them. Its palette striking with aquamarines and vibrant blues, ranging in shade from pale to deep. It is simply breathtaking.

"Do you think the water has some significance? I feel it calling to me," Leora says softly to Aura. Leora can tell that Aura is feeling the same way.

"I bet it does." Aura is mesmerized by the waves. "I'm just not sure what it is yet." Aura's eyes have not yet left the horizon. She feels the pull, too, but there has to be more to this journey.

It isn't going to be easy. One thing she does know

is that they are better together. If this is going to work, they have to work as a team to complete the mission. Aura shakes off the worry and tries to focus on what the others are saying.

In the next few minutes, they devise a plan to break up the island into four sections and explore one at a time all together.

Aura is so proud of Stone for really stepping up. She knows this is a solid plan, and she is ready to follow his lead.

Jett, on the other hand, is definitely not impressed at all. He is not happy about this. He thinks they could get this done a lot quicker if they split up into groups. Well, two groups to be exact. He wants to be with Acacia, and then the rest of them can go be in a group. When he suggests this, he is overruled, which just makes him even madder. He turns on his heels and starts stomping away.

But, as much as Jett seems to hate all of this, he knows deep down that the best plan is to stick together because no one really knows how they are going to get to the next world. But he would never let Stone know that he thinks he is right.

He is also experiencing so much guilt for his and Acacia's part in the collapse that he just wants to help fix it then make his ultimate escape. The emotions of the Selenixies are weighing him down. He wishes they weren't so nice to him. Even when he is pitching a fit, they seem to just joke around about it.

As the group begins to explore, Jett follows behind at a safe distance.

The Selenixies head away from the water. They stand

in the sand, but it is unlike any other they have seen. It has that bronze tone to it and is a mixture of the shell fragments of tiny coquina clams. The beach seems endless.

Up ahead they see dunes, small mounds created by the wind. The dunes are covered in feathery beach grass that is as tall as they are. They make their way through the sea grass. Under their feet was still sand but this sand was different; it was finer, softer sort of.

They try walking north, following the stars. This should be an easy task for them as they love to stargaze and regularly use the stars as a navigational aid, but nothing is really making sense to them lately. It seems like they are hugging the coast because they can still smell the salt in the air.

A short while later, the Selenixies notice a pack of Mermaids playing on the rocks. They are all so excited to see a real-life Mermaid that they rush toward them.

The Mermaids are splashing and laughing, using their tails to flick water at each other. The Selenixies stop to admire their beauty. They are the same size as the Selenixies and have many human features. The Mermaids also have Mystics watching over them.

Each Mermaid is uniquely different. Their tails shimmer in the water. One tail is an electric blue, another a deep green, and the most striking is a deep purple. But they all have prismatic scales. Their hair is as unique as their tail, vibrant red, pink, and orange. Stripes of multi-colored glitter glows in their hair. They are a spectacular sight, and the Selenixies are enchanted by them.

"Stop," states Aura, not really yelling but definitely in

a raised voice. "The Ancient Scrolls say Mermaids can be very playful but are often sinister and like to play tricks. I think I should approach them alone so that they are not alarmed."

"Good idea," says Rocky, giving her a thumbs-up.

"You all stay here and stay hidden. I will go chat with them," whispers Aura.

"No worries, girlie. We got your back," adds Rocky.

Aura flits over and starts chatting with a young Mermaid on the rocks. The two seem to be hitting it off.

From the hiding spot, Stone and Rocky can see that Aura is all good.

"Hi, I'm Aura," Aura says confidently, trying to hide any little bit of trepidation that she has.

"I'm Jewel," says the Mermaid with the purple tail.

Aura, still a little hesitant, asks, "Have you seen anyone that kind of looks like me around?"

Jewel squints and turns her head to the side. "Oh, you're a Selenixie," she says.

"You know who I am?"

"I don't know who you are, but I have heard about the Selenixies from Mystic Chantara. She even showed me pictures. She speaks so fondly of all of you," adds Jewel.

"She does?" Aura answers a little surprised.

"Yes, but I think you might be a little lost. This is not your world. How did you even get here?"

Aura laughs. "You won't believe me if I told you."

"Try me," giggles Jewel.

Aura fills Jewel and the other Mermaids in on all that has happened.

Meanwhile, on the other side of the rocks, Bianca starts to stir. She is not in her perfect little bed with her perfectly fluffy pillows, in her perfect little house. Where she is now, everything looks different. She is not in the forest anymore. This place is warm and squishy and not green at all. She wonders where she is as she flits around looking at the sparkling crystal blue water.

Bianca's long brown hair is pulled back into her signature hairstyle, a high ponytail. Her big brown eyes are framed with long, thick lashes. She is always dressed to play in the next big game. She is what you would call "sporty chic." Sporty, yet sensitive.

How did I get here?

What happened?

Why can't I remember? And why does this place smell so fishy?

She then starts to realize that it is kind of a beautiful place and a glorious day. She is alone, but maybe she just needs some time to relax and find a good spot for yoga. She can figure out the rest later.

And then she sees something moving on the rock near the water in the distance, and she calls out, "Hey! Over here!" Bianca flits a little faster. "Do you know where I am?"

"What are you doing here? This is not your world," says the Mermaid looking a little perplexed.

"I know! I know! I don't know how I got here. I just want to get home." Bianca starts to panic, realizing that even though this is a beautiful place, it doesn't really feel like a mini vacation. On Lumina, there was an overwhelming sense of peace and harmony. And here that feeling is gone and replaced with a sense of dread even though Bianca has not encountered any trouble.

"I don't know how to help you, but I might know someone who can. Follow me."

Pearl swims through the crystal waters until they reach a coral reef speckled with bits of gold where her friend, Jewel, is sitting and chatting with Aura.

Bianca squeals. "OMG, OMG!" She is overcome with joy to see Aura. She flits as fast as she can, barreling into Aura and embracing her in a giant hug.

The two bounce up and down with excitement, so happy to be together.

Jewel explains to Aura and Bianca that when she saw the Selenixies from a distance, she at first thought they were giant birds.

"How funny is that? Us, birds," Bianca chuckles.

"The Mermaids have never seen the Selenixies," adds Jewel.

As for the Selenixies, they had heard stories of a world full of Mermaids but had never actually seen a Mermaid. Well, now they have.

As beautiful as it is here, the Selenixies miss Lumina, and they know they can't stay. They have to try to figure out how to get out of here and get home.

But the beautiful, peaceful feeling of the island is short-lived.

"We have heard from the underwater channels that there are intruders causing trouble on the other side of the island, but we dare not go there. It is ruled by Pirate Pixies, and they are scary," Pearl says.

"Thank you for the information and for taking good

care of our girl Bianca," says Aura, motioning to Stone that it is safe to come out from his hiding spot where they tucked themselves behind a thick patch of beach-grass.

The group of Selenixies heads off in the direction of the Pirate Pixies, figuring that the intruders are probably their friends. But who is causing so much trouble?

"Well, here goes nothing," Jett says to Acacia. "Let's head right for the trouble."

As they explore, the island begins to feel drastically different. The temperature starts to drop, making it just a little bit cooler with each step. The land is gently wilting. All the plants seem to be in duress. Even the sky is turning gray.

A feeling of uneasiness is flooding the Selenixies.

The deeper into the island, the deeper their anxiety. All of the plants and animals feel it too. The island's ashen color creates a weird solemn tone. There is a creepy vibe in the air. The wind whistles through the trees in an eerie way. Like something is out there.

"Oh no, where are we now?" asks Aura.

"Maybe we should have just stayed with the Mermaid," Stone says.

"It was pretty nice there, and the Mermaids seemed nice," adds Aura.

"And now we are somewhere strange and scary," Acacia snarks.

The Selenixies try to hide in a nook of a tree, hoping that no one or nothing saw them. They decide to wait until nightfall to explore.

"We have to do this strategically," says Aura.

"I agree," Stone says.

Nightfall comes and they go out to explore.

Aura gets a tingling feeling up and down her arms. She just knows someone is following them. The hairs on the back of her neck stand on end. There is rustling in the bushes.

"It must be an animal," says Rocky, looking concerned but still trying to be the tough guy.

Then hearing the leaves crunch under their feet, they stop but the sound continues. In unison, they all turn around. But there's nothing there.

"Creepy," whispers Leora.

"Totally," answers Bianca firmly gripping Leora's arm.

The Selenixies start walking again, this time a little faster, trying to get out of where they are. As they move quicker, the other footsteps quicken too.

Leora and Bianca are totally afraid of what is out there.

Aura can feel their hesitation. Being the good leader that she is, Aura realizes that this isn't the right place for them.

"Hey, Stone, why don't you and Rocky go do a little investigating, and I will stay here with everyone else."

"I am going with them. The two scaredy-cats are making my head hurt," says Jett holding his head.

"Fine, let's go then." Stone shakes his head.

"Yo, yo, Jett, you want to fight the bad guys with us?" Rocky jokes.

"I am the bad guy," Jett whispers under his breath.

The trio is on high alert and still feels like they are

being followed. Stone, Rocky, and Jett hatch out a plan to turn on their stalker and surprise them.

One, two, three, they mouth and head straight in the direction of their follower.

They slam into Leo.

"Leo, where did you come from?" asks Stone, startled.

Leo explains to them that he was in the land of the Pirate Pixies. "You will seriously never ever believe me, I barely believe this actually happened," says Leo.

"Dramatic much, like really. I met a friendly spider," says Rocky.

Leo turns his head and looks at him perplexed for the random comment.

"Pirate Pixies," he says.

"You mean pixies?" asks Jett which could be reasonable seeing they just left the Mermaids. "Or pirates?" quickly followed by, "Well we are by the water so it could be possible!"

"No, as I said *Pirate Pixies*," says Leo, laughing because he knows how outlandish it sounds.

"You have to be joking," says Jett, thinking this is a joke.

"No, no, not joking at all, they are tiny but fierce creatures. They have wings the size of their bodies. Their slops or clothing consisted of a canvas doublet and breeches, knitted caps called Monmouth caps, cotton waistcoats and drawers, stockings, linen shirts, and shoes that are all color coordinated for which band of pirates they belong too. Their clothes are very dirty. They have pointy teeth and ears, and they have very long fingers and nails. So gross!" Leo takes a deep breath.

They had captured Leo because he looked different, not like a Pirate Pixie at all.

"The Drake Pirates and the Morgan Pirates are fighting for my custody. They have weapons, and there are a lot of ships, sails, snarls, treasure, and gangplanks. It is crazy!" Leo continues, "I fell out of the sky and landed in the water. When I got to the surface, I was in between two huge ships. And I thought *wow, this is great*, ya know. I have never seen real pirates or real pixies for that matter.

"I thought they were so cool until I was viciously dragged out of the water by my shirt. Before I knew it, I was on the deck of the ship and yelling erupted. The two ships were yelling at each other, saying some not so nice words."

"Why were they yelling?" asks Stone.

"Apparently, they were yelling over me. I couldn't believe it either," says Leo. "Then all of a sudden cannon's were firing. Real cannons. The explosions were so loud!"

Leo makes an explosion sound and the Selenixies jump, like they are actually on the ship.

"The pirates started swinging from one ship to the next holding out their swords. A real and honest and true sword fight. They just kept going and going so I jumped in the water to try to get away. But before I knew it I was dragged out by my shirt again, but this time I was on the other ship!"

"Wow, Leo, this doesn't even seem real," adds Stone not really following what Leo is saying.

"It was totally out of control. I was wrapped up in ropes, and then the other Pirate Pixies tried to get me back to their ship. They put me in a cage in a cargo hold of some sort and I panicked."

"How did you escape?" Stone asks.

"I started hitting the walls and then all of a sudden, the cage opened. I untied myself and snuck out before they could even come talk to me. I dove off the back of the ship and swam and swam and swam and swam until I came ashore. I hid because I didn't know where I was."

"Wow," Jett says, eyes wide.

"This world is crazy." Leo releases a deep breath, shaking his head. "Pirates. I mean, Stone, really, they were real life pirates. I never imagined such chaos—it was pure chaos like you don't understand, you wouldn't understand because you didn't get to see it."

"Sounds like an adventure," Stone laughs, wishing he had been there.

"When I first saw you, I thought I was just seeing things," Leo adds. "But I'm so glad I found you. What happened? How did we get here? I'm hoping you know all the things because this is just way too much for my brain to comprehend all in one shot."

Leo starts shaking like a leaf, traumatized.

"Leo don't worry. You are okay now. We've got ya, dude," says Rocky hugging him in one of his giant bear hugs.

"We are here to help," says Stone, hoping that they won't have to face the pirates.

"I won't go back there," cries Leo, still visibly upset.

"You never have to see those Pirate Pixies again," says Stone, trying to reassure him.

"They are too much for me." Leo starts to settle down.

"Follow us back to where we left Aura, Acacia, Leora, and Bianca. They are waiting for us," says Jett, trying to be helpful.

If Jett hurries them along, they should be able to portal out of there.

"Really? I missed them. I was so scared I was the only Selenixie left. One minute I was eating the most delicious cupcake, and then, bam, I was on a Pirate Pixie boat."

Stone shrugs. "We're not sure."

Jett walks ahead of them hoping to reach the others first to give them the good news. He moves rather quickly; way quicker than Jett ever walks. All of Leo's drama is giving him a headache. So, he is trying to put as much space in between them as he can. He sees Aura and totally gets the idea to take credit for finding Leo, hoping it will make him look like he is a team player.

"I found Leo, I found Leo," Jett calls all proud of himself.

He points toward where Rocky, Leo, and Stone are just coming into view.

The girls jump up and are happy to see him.

"Look who I found," says Jett, presenting Leo to the others.

"Stone filled me in on the way back here." Leo looks straight at Aura and asks, "So, what's up next?"

"Not sure. There must be more Selenixies in this world, or we would have portaled out of here by now," says Aura.

"Maybe we have to swim in the sea," says Leora. "I feel it calling me. It's good for the soul."

"I know, me too," adds Aura, "but I just feel like there may be one more challenge."

"Let's head north and see if it brings us back to the sea," Stone suggests.

And off they go. They decide to flit instead of walk. The farther they head north the colder it gets. The Selenixies are not really used to cold weather. They shiver. Their teeth are chattering. Their wings start to form ice crystals.

"This can't be right," states Acacia.

Jett takes off on his own in another direction.

"Can't he ever just stay with the group? Now we will have to look for him too," Stone complains. "It's too cold to separate. My ankles are starting to hurt. I can't feel my toes. My hands are pulsing. This is ridiculous. I still don't even understand what happened or why we are suddenly facing these challenges. And Jett has to stick with us. We can't separate again."

Stone's anxiety is totally getting to him, and he starts to whine about every little thing which is not the leader he wants to be.

"Yes!" Jett says loud enough for the Selenixies to hear him. He thinks he has figured out a way to get out of this place. "This will bring us home. And everyone will have to bow down to me," he says out loud, totally patting himself on the back.

He stops for a minute to focus, and suddenly he feels a pain down his back. His body is wrapped in a deep ache as everyone's feelings bombard him at once.

Jett picks up his pace to try to outrun the pain. As he runs, the temperature drops and drops. The ground gets harder and harder beneath his feet. The trees are covered in tiny shimmery crystals.

Everything is frozen, a beautiful sight to see. The ice that crusts the snow projects rainbows in every direction. *Nature's prisms*, thinks Jett.

As he's about to turn back, he hears a soft voice calling his name.

"Jett," she whispers. "Jett," she says again.

"Sienna? Is that you?" Jett looks around and tries to follow where the voice is coming from.

"Over here," the soft voice says again.

It sounds kind of like Sienna, but at this point Jett's too scared to know for sure and doesn't want to find out.

"Jett!" cries the voice.

He hears it again, so he turns around, still following the voice, and looks in every direction. He sees Sienna sitting there. She is leaning up against what looks like a giant snowball. She looks injured. *Oh no*, Jett thinks, *now I am going to have to take care of her too. I didn't sign up for this.* And then it clicks, this is the pain he's feeling.

Sienna tells Jett that her wing is hurt and that the cold is not helping. Reluctantly, he helps her try and escape the frozen land. They head out together. Once out of the frozen land, Sienna's wings begin to defrost and start to work again with no pain. It must have been that the temperature was too cold for her wings.

"Ahh," Sienna says. "I feel so much better."

Sienna wants to know the plan now.

Plan? thinks Jett. *My plan does not include Sienna at all. My plan is just for me and Acacia.* Jett thinks quickly on his feet. "Okay, a plan, well we know there are more of us, so the plan is to find the others."

"Sounds good," says Sienna. "But how?"

"The same way I found you, and there is some drama about seven challenges and blah, blah, blah," Jett says. "I am sure Aura will fill you in."

"How many others do you think there are here?" asks Sienna.

Jett is thinking, *OMG, I don't care!* But he says nicely to Sienna, "I don't know, there must be a bunch more." Then he asks Sienna, "How do you think we ended up here?"

She looks at him, perplexed. "I have no idea. I just know I am missing some people."

Jett is trying to feel her out and see if anyone else would think it was them that caused the collapse.

"Don't worry," says Sienna, comforting him.

Jett is not worried. He knows he will find who they still need to find and then they can continue with his plan. He is happy that no one has any idea that he and Acacia are the ones who caused the collapse. Even though he acts tough and says he doesn't care about anyone else, it was not his intention to collapse the whole realm. He was just ready to leave. And he really would be upset if someone ends up hurt because of his actions. He does have a heart, though he hides it well.

Jett and Sienna find their way back to the rest of the group. Everyone is happy to see Sienna. Well, except Acacia. She really has no use for Sienna.

Since the time that they emerged from their pods in the Crystal Fortress, Sienna has tried to befriend Acacia.

Acacia was immediately drawn to and bonded with Jett and simply could not see past him. Sienna looked up to Acacia and was enchanted by her cool demeanor. It's not that Acacia didn't like her, she just didn't see a need for her to always be hanging around Jett trying to steal his attention from her. And she didn't really bring anything to the table, she just always tagged along.

"We have to go to the ocean now," says Leora, demanding the others follow her.

"I feel it, and it is pulling me too. We must go now." Aura hopes this is it.

"I feel it too," says Acacia in disbelief.

"Me too," says Bianca.

"Me too," adds Rocky. "It's crazy. It's so powerful."

"I didn't understand before, but now I need to go too," says Stone, hoping that that's all this feeling is.

"Oh, please." Jett secretly feels it too, so intensely, and much more than he would ever let on.

The powerful draw of the sea leads them all back to the beach and the water's edge.

"We must do this together," says Aura, knowing that together is the only way out of here.

They line up and all grab hands. They head into an oncoming wave. And as the wave rushes over them, they feel refreshed.

"Great job," Mystic Neoma cheers into the optic lens. She is proud of how far they have come in such little time. She bows her head and says words of encouragement. It is like she is whispering to each one of the Selenixies.

Aura hears her words, looks up to the sky, and blows

a single kiss in acknowledgment. When she opens her hand back up there is a Sunstone in it. She places the stone in her pocket. A cloud of yellow glittery stardust starts to swirl around them.

In unison, they all say, "I feel creative and inspired."

Their Selenite is charging more.

The yellow glittery stardust swirls faster, and they portal off into the next land together.

Nine

TRIAL 3: CITY OF JEWELS

As the group lands, they are all a little dizzy. They start looking around, orienting themselves in this new land. The last land was sandy and beachy. Here they feel they are in the clouds. The sky has an odd amber glow to it. They stand on a cliff on the top of a majestic mountain range. They peer out toward the valley that is nestled between the tallest redwoods that anyone has ever seen.

There is a golden glow nestled among the redwoods. From atop the cliff, they can't really see the details of the glow. It just looks like a bright ball with yellow rays shooting out in multiple directions. As they draw closer they see that the city is made up of glowing geometric shapes. Golden cubes, golden spheres, and pyramids all stacked on top of each other. It is a magnificent sight, odd but magnificent.

At the entrance to the city stands four glowing rectangular prisms. The shape of the buildings refracts the light causing rainbows to bounce amongst the golden glow. An interesting city, not something they expected.

But this whole journey is nothing they ever expected. So, it is fun to see what this bejeweled city holds for them.

"There in the distance. Do you see it?" asks Bianca, bathing in the yellowish mist as it envelops her completely. She begins to twirl around and smile.

"It's . . . it's magnificent," adds Acacia, mesmerized by its beauty.

"It must be the City of Jewels," says Aura, beyond excited. "I have read about it in the Ancient Scrolls, but I thought it was just a myth, I didn't think it actually existed."

The Ancient Scrolls describe the City of Jewels as a place where one learns their personal strengths. All who visit the City of Jewels are empowered with confidence and self-esteem. The City of Jewels is said to be a place which creates a life-changing experience.

Up until now, the Selenixies were confident and didn't need to change their lives. But in the middle of this whirlwind which has them questioning everything, the City of Jewels is exactly what they need.

But on the way to the city, Aura and Stone notice a small area that is hidden in the shadows. It's very dark and definitely not inviting. They nod to each other making a mental note to not go anywhere near there.

"That must be it. We must go there," says Leo, pulling them toward the city.

"That's too easy. There must be some obstacles along the way, and I feel like we are still missing some friends. We must look for them first and make the City of Jewels the endgame," says Jett, very sure of himself. He is so self-confident; it is infectious.

He is like a whole different person in this world, and it seems to him that the group is digging his vibe.

For some of the Selenixies, the land feels empowering, but for other Selenixies, the land is making them feel stressed out and anxious. Acacia being one of them; the mist seems to be blocking her emotions while at the same time empowering Jett to be his best self. It is encouraging him to show everyone how amazing he is.

"Umm, okay, yeah, let's do what Jett says," Aura says, stumbling over her words. She gives Stone a little wink, excited to see Jett opening up this way.

"Great idea, Jett," says Stone, trying to regain some control of the situation. "That would be my plan exactly," he continues, unsure of how to really proceed, especially since this is not typical behavior for Jett.

"Don't look so shocked. I do have some good ideas. It's just that you guys don't ever listen to me." Jett throws his head back and chuckles as he walks away.

Stone lets out a little sigh, then laughs with Jett as he motions for all of the Selenixies to follow him. And they do. They are all laughing too.

It is quite evident to all of them that this world is good for Jett, and, in turn, it should be good for them.

Acacia is not loving this land and the effect it has on Jett's personality. He is leading the pack, and that isn't the worst part: he is acting like them on purpose. She is trying to get him aside from all of them to see if he is trying to mess with them. But she is not sure, so she hangs back from the group, hoping he will come to his senses. She is getting farther and farther away from the group when she hears her name.

"Who is calling me?" she mumbles under her breath. She doesn't want to even look. She just wants to get out of this land. She hears the voice again. *Ugh*, thinks Acacia.

"Yo-Yo! Hey, man, is that you?"

Acacia is so confused. The voice is raspy and almost hoarse. Acacia yells, "Hello? Who is this?" She really has no idea, and she really doesn't care.

"It's Magnus," he says in a low whisper.

"What do you want?" asks Acacia a little annoyed.

"Why are you not happy to see me? I thought you would be thrilled," says Magnus, gesturing wildly with his hands. Magnus's buzzed hair is as black as night. His eyes are piercingly black, and it's like he's looking right through Acacia reading her every emotion.

"Yes, yes. I am overjoyed. Blah, blah, blah," says Acacia to appease him. "Why is your voice so low?"

She regrets speaking the words as they come out of her mouth, hoping for a short story.

"I have been hanging with the Giants, and I have to yell so they can hear me," answers Magnus.

He is trying to act cool, because to him Giants are the coolest, and he so wants to be associated with them. He loves Giants because they are super nice to him. They at no point were scared of him or mean to him. When they found him, they knew exactly what he was and invited him to join them and promised to do anything they could to help him find his friends. The Giants are the protectors of the city of jewels. They told him that they knew that his friends would have to come here.

"Giants? Like real giants?" asks Acacia. She is definitely intrigued.

"Yeah, Giants! They are super chill," Magnus adds like it is no big deal. "The Giants were massive. They were the biggest things I have ever seen. I was afraid at first cause ya know they could like squish me and stuff."

Magnus continues, "The Giants are seventy feet tall. But they appear tiny compared to the three hundred-foot redwoods that they live in. They look like you and me, just taller. They live and thrive off nature. Some of them even look like the trees. It is a way of hiding in plain sight. Their hair was leaf green. I had to yell real loud for them to hear me at first," continues Magnus to Acacia, who is only really half listening. She is intrigued by the Giants, but she's worried about Jett's new behavior.

"This one Giant, Ted, picked me up and put me on his shoulder, I felt like I was floating in the clouds. It was the absolute coolest thing. Then we climbed a mountain, in like two steps. We sat on top like it was a stool. The Giant's hands were enormous, like the size of the moon. And his legs were the size of tree trunks. But one thing I will tell you, their breath stinks bad. Also, I want to know where they find clothes that fit them."

Acacia has some questions but doesn't want to seem too eager. She and Jett read about the Giants in the Ancient Scrolls and always wanted to know more.

"Yeah, yeah but why did you say they were so chill?" says Acacia with a laugh trying to act like she is just making conversation.

"Well, they made some funny jokes, and loved acting a bit goofy. And at night they danced and sang around the campfire. They took lots of naps, like they just laid down on the peaks of the mountains and went to sleep, so cool." Magnus beams at how cool he thinks his story is.

"OMG, we need to get out of here. I gotta go tell Jett," says Acacia.

"Jett is here? That is awesome!" says Magnus, excited to see his friend.

"Yeah, whatever. Follow me," says Acacia reluctantly. This might be her ticket out of this place. Acacia races in the direction of where she thinks the group is headed. She starts to yell for them.

"Hey, hey! Look! Look who I found. Now off to the City of Jewels we go," she yells, hoping they will all just follow her so this can be the end of it all.

Everyone is so excited to see Magnus. He loves the attention. He fills them in on some funny stories about his time with the Giants.

Acacia is in a major rush, trying desperately to push them toward the City of Jewels.

"I get that you are in a rush, but I think there is more to do. I don't think we are done yet," says Aura, trying to be patient with Acacia.

In Lumina as well as the other world, the sky was crystal blue. But in this world the sky has a yellow glow to it, like a fog enveloping them. In some places the yellow foggy haze is thick and other places it is very thin and whispery. The haze also seems to be changing some of the Selenixies' personalities. It is bringing out the best in some and the worst in others.

"Maybe you're not done, but I am," proclaims Acacia.

She looks like she is going to burst into tears. "Let's get out of here. This is not my favorite place. The yellow haze is making me crazy. I feel blocked, and I don't like it one bit."

"We must continue on our journey and look for others," adds Jett confidently.

This just makes Acacia even madder. She rolls her eyes.

"I know this is hard for you. You just have to trust me that I got this," says Jett winking at her.

Acacia turns and stomps away, frustrated with his attitude.

"What's with her?" he adds, totally oblivious.

Meanwhile, unbeknownst to the Selenixies, there is a very dark side to this crazy world. Something like they have never experienced. They unknowingly head right for it. They are on the outside of the Land of the Goblins when they start to notice that everything is dead. All the trees and flowers are brown and wilted. The ground is a deep shade of brown. There are no animals or chirping birds. The air is filled with doom and gloom. You can feel the negative pressure in the air. A dust filled wind rustles the leaves and blows through the area.

Aura and Stone had read about the Land of the Goblins in the Ancient Scrolls. They never truly believed that they were real as the stories of them were so horrific. They could never imagine a land that was dead. A place where nothing grew. A place where the sun never shone. A place that was always gray and smelled of burning brush. A place that could make you feel so miserable.

The Selenixies are starting to feel the dread here. They

cannot fathom that a place like this exists. Lumina was so lush and full of color and life, this is the exact opposite.

"This cannot be good," says Bianca, shaking like she has the chills.

"I am scared," says Leora, grabbing onto Rocky and Aura's arms. She is trying to hide behind them.

"Hold up," says Stone. "Hey, Jett, how about you and I go explore?" Stone figures that Jett will love this idea and that there will be no argument.

"Yeah, that's a great idea, Stone," says Jett. "I was thinking the same thing."

The others are looking at each other confused, like really is this happening? It has to be a dream. Jett is always so disagreeable. The fact that he has been so agreeable and thinks it is a great idea is puzzling.

"I am coming too," states Aura. She thinks she might be able to help.

"Sounds like a plan. I will just sit here until you heroes get back to save us," snarks Acacia, looking straight at Jett. Acacia fully knows that Jett is going to hate it there. He feels everything, and it's gonna be painful, but she is letting him be. And she will laugh about it later.

"Yes, yes, the heroes," Jett says with a huge smile on his face.

Little does the group know, but Cassius is already there in the Land of the Goblins searching for a way out. It is just to the right side of the City of Jewels. Cassius is wandering around and notices that this place is super spooky, and he can feel the presence of others. It is worrying him a bit. He is not sure if they are friend or foe.

"This is not going to be good. Not at all. But I'm good," Cassius says, trying to convince himself. I do know how to get out of here."

Of course, he knows exactly where he is. He knows everything about everything.

Cassius will never actually admit he is lost.

"To the right," he says. "No, to the left will be best."

Everywhere he looks is just dead. There's no other way to describe it. A feeling of dread washes over him. He can't stay here. All the trees and flowers are crumbled and dried out.

He is looking for some light or a glimmer of hope. Like if he keeps walking he will be able to be right back in glorious Lumina and this will all be a bad dream. But he is here now and starting to feel the effects of this place on his heart.

"I think . . ." Cassius is starting to freak out a little, but thankfully he is alone and no one else can see how scared he is. "I must be in the world of the super creepy trolls or something," he says quietly, not wanting to attract any attention.

Everything here is weird and dirty. Not his thing at all. But it is no biggie. He will take a quick look around and then try to find someone. Not knowing who he is supposed to be looking for doesn't help either. But he just has to keep pretending he has this all under control. "No problems at all," he whispers. He is definitely intimidated, but he wants to remain cool and calm.

He heads toward the darkest area to try to prove to himself that he is tough and can handle anything. "Yup. No one here. I am so getting out of here."

He is about to run in the opposite direction as fast as he can, but he stops when he feels something. He decides to flit up, heading to the right, then to the left. Then he stops. "How is the feeling beneath me?" He floats down to the ground, and there is a small cave. He starts to walk in.

"Okay, Cassius, be as quiet as you can," he reminds himself. He tiptoes through the cave. The cave is dark, and it looks very deep, like it goes on for miles. "I am definitely not going in that far."

Cassius comes across a pile of what looks like dead leaves.

Oh, he thinks. *Maybe that's nothing.* He turns to leave, but then trips on a stick and stumbles forward.

"Oh, no," he yells out. "Oh, sugar. Cassius, be quiet."

"Cassius? Cassius, is that you?" asks Zira. Zira's voice seems shaky and scared. She starts to sit up from her hiding spot.

"Who is that?" asks Cassius. Now he is secretly freaking out.

"It's Zira." She sounds so scared and is hiding under the dead leaves.

Zira's long blonde hair is perfectly straight, although a bit tousled at the moment, and is long, like long to her waist long. Her blue eyes gleam against her black lined eyes and thick black lashes, but if you look close enough into them, you can see her fear.

"Zira, it's okay to come out," he reassures her. He mentally pats himself on the back since he totally knew he would find someone here.

"Oh, Cassius, how did you get here? This is a terrible

place," cries Zira. She's a mess, all dirty, and with leaves in her hair.

Cassius is shocked to see Zira so scared. That is generally not her style. "What's your drama? It's not so bad here."

"You have no idea," she says, her voice shaky. "This is the Land of the Goblins. They are terrible little green creatures, and we must leave here before they come back." She clings to his arm.

"I don't think it can be that bad, but let's go. Grab my hand, and we'll just run." He does not appreciate the clinginess.

She appears skeptical at first, but she follows his lead, and they start running.

Cassius and Zira come running out of the cave on the south side of the Land of the Goblins and are greeted by Sienna and Acacia.

Sienna is so excited to see Zira and Cassius. She cares very deeply for all the Selenixies. Before Sienna can even say a word, Cassius is rehashing the whole story, painting himself as the hero.

"I'm glad Cassius found you, Zira," Sienna says, trying to act tough. Shrugging, Sienna turns to Acacia, expecting something from her.

Acacia says nothing and just rolls her eyes and goes to find Jett.

Zira is telling Sienna about all the things in this scary world that she just experienced.

"I can't even explain to you this world. It was, it was insane. These little Goblins," says Zira.

"Goblins? What are Goblins?" Sienna asks.

"They are these tiny little green sticky creatures with these big red bulging bloodshot eyes. They are the scariest things I've ever seen in my life, and it seems like they had this constant stream of snot coming out of their noses. Like could you ever?" says Zira totally grossed out.

"Oh my gosh, they sound horrible," Sienna agrees scrunching her face in disgust.

"Horrible doesn't even cut it and all they did was run around, I mean like run fast like zip here and zip there," Zira continues.

"Did you try to talk to them?" questions Sienna.

"I tried very hard to communicate with them but all they could do was scream. They were so angry, and I don't know what they were really angry about," scoffs Zira.

"Wouldn't you be angry too if you lived amongst dead trees and rotting leaves and a gray world that just looked putrid at all times?" Cassius interjects.

"I guess, but they didn't have to be that angry and mean," Zira replies, rolling her eyes at Cassius's condescending comment.

"Did they hurt you?" asks Sienna with genuine concern.

"No, they didn't hurt me. Well, they did pull my hair and they threw dirt at me. They just really scared me, and that's why I was hiding because I just didn't wanna be around them. I didn't see any way of getting out of the land, so I just hid so that they would leave me alone," explains Zira, visibly shaken.

"I think you're overreacting. I don't think it was that bad. I didn't hear any of the screaming. I think you're making that up. I think you just need to get over it and move on," mocks Cassius, brushing her off.

"Well in my eyes, Zira, it sounds really scary and I'm happy that you're safe now and that you never have to go back to that world," says Sienna, assuring Zira with a pat on the shoulder.

"I am so happy that you found me and that am no longer in that scary place. Cassius, you were not there. You didn't have these green slimy things up in your face screaming at you and trying to scare you. They were nose to nose with me and screaming so loud that it hurt my ears. I was very afraid, and no one should have to be that scared. They yanked my hair and threw dirt on me. So, you know what, Cassius? You can think whatever you want, but you don't know what truly happened," says Zira.

And, in true Cassius style, he just starts talking over Zira, like he knows everything about what really happened.

"Oh, stop it. It isn't that bad. I wouldn't go back, but at no time was I scared or feared for my life, you know. It just isn't my cup of tea. It is dark and dirty. And kinda dead. But still, it isn't as bad as Zira is making it out to be," blurts out Cassius trying to be tough even though he was actually terrified and desperate to be back on Lumina himself.

He is acting so self-righteous it is annoying. Cassius has always been a bit of a "know-it-all," so the girls just let him ramble while they walk away.

Cassius doesn't realize they left. He keeps talking and talking, and by the time he pauses the girls are gone.

"Hey! Where did you all go?" asks Cassius, searching for his friends.

Cassius takes off to find someone else to tell his adventures to.

Meanwhile, Sienna and Zira corner Acacia and Jett.

"Ugh! These two are so annoying," mumbles Acacia to Jett.

Jett begins to ask Zira some questions about her experience.

"Were you able to understand them?" Jett is wondering what language the Goblins were speaking.

"No, no, not at all. They just sound like they are screaming a lot," says Zira.

Jett scratches his head. "Hmm, that's interesting."

Acacia is getting a headache. *These two need to stop talking*, she thinks.

"Why is this bothering me so much? I don't understand. Normally I couldn't care less. But it really annoys me. This stinks," Acacia mumbles under her breath hoping no one hears her. She tries really hard to focus on something else. But nothing is working.

"I think it's time," says Aura to the group. She is visibly excited. "I feel like we need to make our way to the City of Jewels now."

"I think this is the right time too," says Stone. "If we travel through the night we should be there in the morning."

"Perfect time for a sunrise yoga session," says Bianca, with a glowing smile.

"Oh, Bianca, is that all you think about?" asks Leora teasingly.

"Priorities, priorities," adds Bianca with a chuckle.

Acacia is so excited that they are heading to the City of Jewels and is hoping this journey will get them out of this yucky world. She cannot wait to leave, and so she begins herding everyone along.

Jett leads the charge. Off to the City of Jewels they go.

The City of Jewels ends up being a lot closer than they thought, and they arrive rather quickly.

It is still night, and they are not a hundred percent sure what they need to do next. They do some exploring but are all truly exhausted from the day's events. As a group they decide to settle somewhere, hoping there will be more clarity in the morning.

Cassius finds a good spot for them to bed down for the night.

They all stay close together, but Acacia is keeping her distance as usual, and Zira and Sienna are not too far from Cassius and Magnus. They all look over at Jett basking in the yellow haze, even at night, and they look at each other and agree quietly that this has changed Jett, and they can't wait to leave.

While half of the group loves this version of Jett, his old crew, Cassius, Magnus, Zira, Sienna, and especially Acacia, want the old Jett back as fast as possible.

Jett, however, cannot get enough of this world. He's never felt better. Here, he feels like he has total control of his empathy. He is still feeling everyone's drama, but he is able to handle it. It isn't so overwhelming and crippling. He wants to stay here forever. He hopes that this feeling stays with him.

As the sun begins to rise, they all start to feel this sense of calm and peace as they awaken.

They decide to walk into the center of the City of Jewels.

They are all completely mesmerized but its beauty. The walls sparkle with every color of the rainbow. The larger jewels encrusting the wall make it the most exquisite thing they have ever seen. It is like the entire place has been sprinkled in glitter. They are in awe.

They are still confused though. They gather in the center and all face outward, waiting.

"This must be where we are supposed to be," says Aura. She can feel Neoma watching and knows this is the spot.

"How do you really know? You're just guessing," snarks Acacia.

"This is a mess," says Sienna, totally trying to support Acacia.

"OMG, stop! She has not steered us wrong yet," says Jett, sticking up for Aura for the first time ever.

"There is a first time for everything," says Acacia, as she turns on her heel and walks in the other direction.

"Stop, please. Stop and look," says Leora pointing to the sky. She is glowing.

When the sun reaches the top of the sky, a ray of sunlight shines down directly at them.

Aura again hears Mystic Neoma's voice cheering them on. She blows a single kiss in acknowledgment to the sky. When she opens her hand, there is a Sunstone in it. She places it in her pocket with the other gems.

A green glittery mist appears.

They say in unison, "I can accomplish incredible things."

Recharging more, their Selenite is getting stronger.

Then the green glittery mist envelops them and portals them off.

Ten

MYSTICAL MYSTICS

Since the collapse of the Crystal Fortress, something that no one even believed was possible, the Mystics have been glued to the optic lens following the Selenixies every step of the way. The sisters are very invested in how these trials will play out. They have never seen anything like this before. This is all very new to them. They are not sure what to do and how they can help. Especially when the Goddess Selene showed up in the Mystics plane.

Initially, Selene is so distraught, sobbing that this was never supposed to happen. Selene had thought she created the most perfect world and the most perfect creatures. She never thought that something evil could ever darken their world. After much thought and tears, she created a plan for them to recharge and rejuvenate the fortress. It isn't going to be easy. But it will make the Selenixies stronger than ever.

She spends some time with the Mystics laying out the plan, making them fully understand the importance of the seven trials. When she finishes, she tells the Mystics that by no means could they help them in any way.

"Neoma, Aura will come to you in a dreamlike state, and you will only be able to tell her the basics of what is going to happen. They need to figure it out on their own. I have faith that they will be able to complete the trials," states Selene very confidently.

"As you wish, Selene," answers Mystic Neoma, unsure of all the information that the Mystics just received.

Selene continues to tell them that they can cheer them on from afar, but they cannot help them. She gave the Mystics the crystals that the Selenixies need to power up the grid. The crystals are the only thing they can give them after they complete a trial. This should encourage them to keep going.

After the third land, the Mystics are beaming with pride over the Selenixies' progress. Yes, Neoma is the Mystic assigned to them, but their love for the Selenixies is as deep as they come. Each of them has a very specific assignment, but all the sisters are all connected and intertwined.

"I can't believe they have gotten this far this fast. They are so amazing," squeals Mystic Neoma gleaming and spinning in a circle creating a ribbon effect with her deep purple dress.

The Mystics huddle around the optical lens, all feeling a mix of emotions.

"But the hardest part has yet to come," adds Mystic Brisa, her sparkling sky-blue eyes filled to the brim with tears. Sometimes her emotions get the best of her. She gently wipes them away, using her scarf.

"Let's see how they do in the Land of Love," Mystic Lana says as she twirls her light auburn hair.

"This land is all about recharging and rejuvenating the love they all feel for each other but sometimes don't acknowledge," says Mystic Neoma. "I am worried about the next land, the Dungeon of Darkness." As a space element, Mystic Neoma is deeply connected with Selenixies' inner wisdom, intuition, and fears.

Everything in nature is made up of five elements or the five Mystics: Lana Earth, Chantara Water, Seraphina Fire, Brisa Air, and Neoma Spirit.

Mystic Lana is grounding and calming. She is loyal and very dependable. But she is practical to a fault.

Mystic Chantara has the ability to flow, adapt, and bind. She is charming and refreshing. But she can be mysteriously private and overly emotional.

Mystic Seraphina is a cleanser. She burns up toxins and impurities. She is strong and enthusiastic. But also, temperamental and passionate.

Mystic Brisa channels clear communication and self-expression. She is creative and fun, but also overly adventurous.

Mystic Neoma acts as the container for all the other elements and is the element from which all other elements originate, and to which they all return. She is levelheaded and balanced. But she can be overwhelmed with the pressure she is faced with and tends to worry.

Mystic Neoma is speaking under her breath. Pacing back and forth in front of the lens, like she is fighting an internal battle.

"Hey, no stop. Neoma, you can't. Ugh this is so frustrating," she mumbles.

"Shhh . . . don't give them any clues. They have to find out on their own," says Mystic Brisa. "They will have to rely on their communication skills to succeed."

"I just want what's best for them." Mystic Neoma sighs. She is so frustrated that she can't help.

"Don't fret. They will find the right path, and it will make them stronger," says Mystic Seraphina, confidently. Her fire engine red hair seems illuminated.

"Teamwork makes the dream work," adds Mystic Chantara with a sparkle in her turquoise blue eyes as she flows a bubble of water back and forth between her hands. Her skin is a pearly shade, almost luminescent.

The Mystics each glow in their own ways.

"I know, I know. They are the Selenixies, and they will always do what is best for all of them," adds Mystic Neoma.

The Selenixies are known for their love for each other. Deep down they will always do what is best for all of them. This is displayed in the way they live their daily lives. They rely on each other. Their lives are intertwined and interconnected on every level. They work and play in a harmonious way. Even when there is drama within the group, they work together to resolve the issues. The Selenixies understand that just because they may not love an idea that it maybe be the best idea for the group as a whole and for their world. They understand that sometimes you don't always get what you want and that it is okay. They also understand that it may be upsetting to them to not get their way but to not dwell in it. A happy life is the life you make. They don't sweat the small stuff and try to live their best lives.

"But I just wish, ugh, I could guide them more," Mystic Neoma says.

"Neoma, they have to do this on their own. It is their lesson to learn," cautions Mystic Brisa.

"They will not be able to resurrect the Crystal Fortress if we help them," adds Mystic Lana. She can see in her sister's eyes that she desperately wants to help and join the beloved Selenixies on their journey.

"I know, I know, but it is in my nature to help," says Mystic Neoma.

"It is in all of our natures to want to help, but they must rely on each other and strengthen their bond," states Mystic Lana.

"I am going to meditate for a bit." Mystic Neoma tears herself away from the optic lens.

Eleven

TRIAL 4: LAND OF LOVE

Chantal is gently woken up by the flutter of butterfly wings against her skin. She slowly opens her eyes. She lets out a giant yawn, the kind of yawn that happens after a restful night of sleep. Chantal is startled to see that she is no longer in Lumina, but she is pleasantly surprised by the beauty that is all around her.

She has landed on what looks like an exquisite pink rose. She can't be one hundred percent sure until she climbs out of it, of course. But to her, at this moment, that is what it looks like and smells like. And, oh the smell. It is glorious! She tells herself that when she returns home, she will plant a field of pink roses so she can bask in the beautiful aroma every day.

But first, she has to figure out what just happened and where everybody is. It is very strange to be without all the other Selenixies. She is not afraid at all, but she starts to worry a little that she may be all alone. She tries to concentrate on the others, but she feels nothing, which is so weird because she can always tell who is around. Right now, all she feels is empty.

Everything is going to be okay. She will figure this out. She starts to believe that there is something bigger than her going on here. She feels the love that the Universe has for them and knows that it will protect them and make sure that what is meant to be is meant to be. She trusts the power of the divine and has ultimate faith in it.

She thinks that she should be sad, but she isn't. She thinks there has to be a reason the Universe separated everyone.

"I will get to the bottom of this," she says out loud to no one.

This is typical Chantal behavior.

She gently slides from the pink rose to the ground, hoping to get a better view of where she is. Everything looks very big. Everything is vividly colored. It is the most stunning thing she has ever seen. Other than Lumina of course. There are fields as far as the eye can see of beautiful, lush roses and peonies in every shade of pink and red and white. The flowers are endless. They seem to touch the sky. Everything is so dynamic. The air is electric, and the vibrations are intense.

As she is busy admiring the landscape and feeling all the feels, a gigantic monarch butterfly lands beside her. They aren't too different in size. Everything in this land is supersized.

The monarch speaks. Chantal takes it as a blessing that this beautiful butterfly wants to speak to her.

"You must be Chantal," says the butterfly wistfully.

"I am. And who might you be?" asks Chantal in her sweetest voice.

"My name is Holly, and we have all been waiting for you to wake up," says Holly.

"How long have I been sleeping?" asks Chantal.

"A day or so," says the butterfly. "We were all quite startled when you arrived. You burst into our world and landed with a great thud."

"A great thud? That sounds frightening. I am so sorry that I upset you in any way. It was not my intention," says Chantal, a little embarrassed.

"We know. It was actually a little exciting. Stuff like that doesn't really happen here," giggles Holly. "It's not every day that a Selenixie falls from the sky."

"How do you know who I am?"

"Everyone knows who you are. You are one of the famous Selenixies."

"Oh, I must apologize. You know about me, but I know nothing about you," Chantal says sadly.

"No worries. We were all so excited that you landed here and that we would get to meet you," adds Holly.

"I am happy I landed here too. And now I get to know you all, too," says Chantal. "You keep saying we. Who's we?"

"Well, there are the butterflies, and the ladybug clan, and the grasshopper crew, and I can't forget the bees. Oh, Queen Bee is going to love you," Holly says.

"And they all talk like you do?" questions Chantal.

Holly laughs. "Of course, we do."

"Just checking. So, what are we waiting for? Let's go meet them," Chantal says excitedly.

So, off they flit, flying together to make a formal introduction. Everyone is very excited to meet her, and at times they are all talking at once. Chantal is still so taken aback by this whole experience, that she never actually asks where she is.

And then an entourage of enormous bees steps forward, and everyone stops in their tracks.

"The queen is here," announces an army of bees.

The bees part into two straight lines that lead right to Chantal.

Chantal looks up to see the queen bee heading toward her.

When the queen reaches her, Chantal curtsies, and softly says, "How do you do, Your Majesty?"

"Hello, my sweet," says the queen. "It is ever so nice to meet you."

"It is nice to meet you too," gushes Chantal. "I have never met a queen bee."

"I have never met a Selenixie. I have heard wonderful things about them and their land, but until now, I have never had the pleasure of meeting one," states the queen happily.

"Can I ask you a question, Your Majesty?"

"Of course, my dear, yes."

"Where is here? I have never been off Lumina and didn't know anywhere but Lumina really existed."

"You are in the Land of Love. It is a majestic place filled with love and understanding," says Queen Bee. "The Land of Love welcomes you with open arms."

Suddenly two worker bees approach the queen.

She takes a step back from Chantal to speak with them.

Chantal tries hard to listen without being obvious, but she cannot hear their very soft voices.

The queen looks pleasantly surprised as she listens to the other bees. After a minute or two she steps back to Chantal.

"Your fellow Selenixies have just arrived," states Queen Bee.

Chantal's whole face lights up.

"Wait, what? They are here? Oh, I can't believe it! Where? I need to go to them," Chantal says excitedly.

"You will, but not just yet. They need some time to figure something out. It looks like you were sent here on some sort of journey," adds the queen.

"But shouldn't I be with them on this journey?"

"They need to realize how much they love each other. Everyone knows how much you love them, but they sometimes forget how much they truly love each other."

"Oh, okay," says Chantal, a little disappointed that she can't go to them right away.

"We can send them help, though. I have a great idea. Let's send them clues to remind them of how much they love one another," says Queen Bee.

"How?" asks Chantal. "I will do anything to help them."

The queen thinks about it for a minute. Then they look at each other and know exactly how to help them.

Meanwhile, on the other side of the Land of Love, the Selenixies are starting to explore this new land. As they look around, all they can see is green. All different shades, in every direction. But it really isn't what they are seeing, it is what they are all feeling. This whole land is about feelings. And now, their feelings of love are overwhelming. Absolutely overwhelming. For most of them, this world brings a wonderful feeling. Being filled with complete love for someone else is a terrific feeling. For others, that feeling of love can be quite the opposite.

The overwhelming feeling made Jett feel uncomfortable inside. It is too much. "Ugh!" says Jett. "How do we get out of here?"

Jett whispers to Acacia his plan for them to get away from this all too loving place. Jett's feelings are being enveloped by this beautiful love, and since he is so empathic, it is scaring him a bit. He feels completely overtaken by a loving feeling, and so he freezes. It's not that he is afraid of love, he felt lots of love in the City of Jewels. It's just in this land, there is ONLY love and it's not balanced for him. He is scared and afraid, so he turns the toughness on.

Acacia, on the other hand, is basking in the love, enjoying the feeling she is experiencing. This is the complete opposite from the way she felt in the City of Jewels. So, for her, this world is great, and it is giving her this weird feeling of complete happiness.

"Sure, Jett," Acacia smiles, "whatever you want, sweetie. We can leave whenever you are ready. But I just don't understand why you want to leave all our loving friends."

She is humoring Jett and just saying yes to him so she can bask in love and not deal with drama. She doesn't want anyone to ruin this feeling.

"I think we need to head to the west. It looks like there may be something in that direction," says Stone, looking off in the distance.

"Great idea," answers Aura, who trusts Stone's intuition.

"Yup, yup. Like always, let's follow the almighty Stone," barks Jett.

"Exactly," says Cassius, coming to Jett's side.

Jett wants to be the leader and have everyone do his bidding. He doesn't fully get that being a good leader is thinking about the group before yourself. Jett just wants to be in charge thinking that it will quiet the emotions, and everyone will leave him alone.

Cassius looks up to Jett so he goes along with what he says, hoping to win Jett's approval.

"Not this again," says Rocky. "If you have a better idea, let's hear it."

"I am so sick of all this fighting," says Acacia. "Let's all try to work together."

"I so agree with Acacia," says Aura.

Acacia is beaming ear to ear. She really wants to be friends with Aura, but she just doesn't know how.

"Okay, okay. West it is. I am too tired to argue with all of you. Lead the way, our righteous leader," Jett adds in a mildly snarky tone in Stone's direction.

Jett's heart is still overwhelmed and if he doesn't protect it with sarcasm, he's afraid it might actually burst on the spot.

They start walking and find themselves in a field of roses.

"I miss Chantal," says Bianca out of nowhere.

"Me too," adds Sienna.

"She really brought us all together," adds Leo.

"I hope we find her soon," says Zira sadly.

"I don't want to do this without her," adds Aura.

Chantal can hear them talking, but she is too far away to reach them.

"I want to be with you too," she cries. This is a new power for Chantal, gifted to her in her time of need to know she is not alone. She will soon be reunited with the Selenixies.

Queen Bee, seeing how upset she is, sits her down and starts to ask about her friends and their life on Lumina.

"Well," says Chantal, "I have so much to tell you. Where should I start?"

"First tell me which Selenixies are here," asks the queen curious about the others.

"There is Aura and Stone, Jett and Acacia, and of course Bianca, Leo, and Lenora. Oh, and Zira, Sienna, Magnus, and Casius. And how could I forget Rocky. You will love Rocky, everyone does." Chantal relaxes a bit as she remembers her besties.

Seeing the change in Chantal's demeanor Queen Bee continues to ask about the Selenixies in hopes to provide comfort and show as much love as she can.

"Why don't you share some stories with us?" says the queen. "Your stories will help us get to know them and love them as much as you do."

"That is a wonderful idea," says Chantal. She is so excited to share stories about her friends. "Aura is brave and kind. She'll absolutely do anything for you. One time, our friend Sienna was having the hardest time collecting oranges from the fruit trees. It was her turn to harvest them, and for some reason, there were so many that season. Way too much for one Selenixie. Aura saw her struggling and dropped what she was doing to help. She told Sienna that it was always okay to ask for help and that this was an abnormally large harvest. She told her what a great job she was doing and how proud she was of her. It made Sienna not feel like she couldn't do it on her own and that sometimes you just need a little help from your friends. I love that about Aura."

As Chantal finishes telling the story, a large bubble filled with that memory floats across the Land of Love to the Selenixies, and they can hear and see it too.

As a giant bubble starts to approach them, the sky turns a rich shade of emerald around it, creating the perfect contrast for the memory. They are all so intrigued by its content they look up as the bubble is growing larger. It reaches them and they watch the memory play out in the green sky.

They all stand there looking up in awe of the scene playing out in front of them. It is the most amazing thing they have ever seen.

Sienna shares a smile with Aura. It is a happy memory for both of them, and thinking about that moment starts to pull the group a little closer together.

"Oh, let's talk about Bianca next," suggests Queen Bee.

"Bianca is super laid-back. She is my absolute favorite meditation partner. She is very in tune with nature. And she really shines when she is leading a yoga session. She tries very hard to help you relax and fully involve yourself in your practice. She is always available to help realign yourself with the Universe and center your inner being. This is all very important for a happy life," gushes Chantal.

As the bubble blows, they can see Bianca leading them in a yoga practice and smiling to the sky.

They all start to laugh. It is so representative of Bianca.

"Just don't ask her to collect lavender," teases Aura.

Bianca chuckles remembering the time she was tasked with collecting lavender and sat down to meditate before starting and ended up napping the day away among the relaxing lavender aroma. She couldn't be found for hours until she just showed up in the center of the Crystal Fortress covered in purple flowers.

Their hearts fill as one loving memory sparks another one and another one.

"I want to talk about Jett," says the queen. "He seems like he has many layers, a tough one."

"Well, he is on the outside," says Chantal. "But on the inside, he is a mushy teddy bear."

Chantal shares about the time Jett came to visit her in her house as she was baking sweet treats for the full moon festival.

"I was in full on baking mode and there was flour and sugar flying everywhere. I was dancing and singing, and Jett walked in with a special delivery. He was not happy at first that he was tasked with the delivery, but he came in with a grumpy look on his face. And then I did what no one else would really do. I threw flour at him. Oh boy, was he surprised. He gasped. But come on, what did he expect, coming all grumpy into my house? Well, I was not expecting him to pick up a handful and throw it back at me. And that started the most exciting flour fight I was ever in. My house was completely covered, but it was so much fun. Well, we laughed and laughed at the shenanigans going on in my kitchen. Then I baked his favorite brownies, and we spent the rest of the afternoon cleaning up and chatting about everything under the moon. It was the day that I saw all the love that Jett's heart had to give. It is my most fond memory of him," says Chantal with a tear in the corner of her eye.

"That is a great memory," adds the queen, smiling sweetly at Chantal.

As the bubble memory reaches the group it makes them all really smile to see the softer side of Jett.

At first, Jett shakes his head in disbelief and claims, "I am so not a teddy bear." But as the story progresses, Jett smirks a half smile and says to the sky, "Anything for you, Chantal."

As the Selenixies approach the hive more and more bubbles pass by, each with amazing memories of all the fun they have had together, reminding them of all their love.

Queen Bee stands, and the army flanks her side.

"It is time," she says rather regally.

"Time? Time for what?" questions Chantal.

"Time for you to rejoin your friends. Their hearts are full, and the only thing left for them to do in the Land of Love is to reunite with you, sweet Chantal."

Chantal can't contain her excitement.

"Go now. The butterflies will lead the way," orders the queen.

And with that, a flood of butterflies scoops Chantal up and leads her right to the Selenixies.

The group looks up to the sky and sees this beautiful sight of hundreds of butterflies. There are all different species flying toward them. It looks so majestic.

As they are all admiring the sight, Chantal steps out in front of them. With the sunshine at her back and butterflies all around, she looks like an angel. It takes them a second to realize it is really her and not just a dream.

"Chantal, is that you?" Jett calls.

She starts running to him, and he opens his arms to her. She leaps into them.

"I am so happy to see you all," cries Chantal with happy tears.

A teal glittery mist starts to appear. Aura gets that feeling again and hears Mystic Neoma's voice in her head telling her to keep going. She looks up to the sky and blows a single kiss in acknowledgment. When she opens her hand, there is a Rose Quartz in it. She places it in her pocket.

As they all embrace in the biggest—and first ever—group hug, they all say in unison, "I love and accept myself and others."

Charging, charging, charging, their Selenite is restoring.

Then, the glittery mist swirls faster, enveloping them as they are whisked away in a cloud of teal glitter.

Twelve

TRIAL 5: DUNGEON OF DARKNESS

The Mystics are glued to the optic lens, with worried looks on their faces.

"This is it, this is the trial I was worried about," says Mystic Neoma.

"It will be okay, they are together now, they will be able to do great things," adds Mystic Lana.

"This is something that they have never experienced," says Mystic Brisa.

"The darkness will make them rely heavily on their other senses," Seraphina states.

They all reach out for each other's hands and surround the optic lens anxiously waiting for the next trial to begin.

With all of the Selenixies still feeling so euphoric after their time in the Land of Love, they are caught off guard by being dropped into complete darkness. At first, they are excited for their next adventure.

They quickly gather together and start to look for light. It takes a few minutes, but no one can find any light. This does not make sense to them. Their eyes start to adjust slightly. They can see each other's faces but not much more than that.

"Where are we?" questions Aura, squinting to see in the dark. "Why is it so dark?"

"Are we outside?" questions Bianca.

"Wouldn't there be stars if we were outside?" Leo wonders.

Everyone is so confused.

"How did this even happen?" asks Sienna, feeling around for something, not really sure what she is looking for.

"It feels like we are trapped," states Zira.

There was a large bang followed by a weird gurgling sound. It was nothing they have ever heard before.

"What did we do to deserve this?" Bianca feels around in the dark. "We have never done anything wrong, what do you want?"

Another bang, then some weird howling sound comes from one of the tunnels.

They are all frightened. It is so cold and so damp and so eerie. They have never experienced a place like this. And now, somehow, they are trapped. They are all shivering.

They try to stay as close to each other as possible, unsure of this new land. Quickly, they realize that maybe togetherness is not the best option.

They are all talking at once, but no one is listening at all. Everyone is talking over each other. It is a mishmash of voices and words, but nothing is making any sense.

They start to get frustrated with each other.

And then the fighting begins. Yelling, talking over each other, stomping. Loud and angry fighting. And this is a fight like they have never fought before. They all have had different opinions during moments through the years. And they don't always see eye to eye. But this is different. It is an epic fight.

"This way!" shouts Aura.

"Do we go?" asks Stone.

"Maybe, I think not," yells Cassius.

"No, no, this way," demands Magnus.

Everyone has something to say all at once.

Voices grow louder and louder to the point that everyone is screaming.

"Wait, why is this happening," says Zira, confused by all the tension.

"I understand why some of you deserve this, but not me," declares Leora, acting all high and mighty, which is totally not her thing.

"Really? Really, Leora you're so perfect," says Magnus sarcastically in a rather nasty tone.

"Not perfect, but better than you," adds Bianca, sticking up for Leora.

"Wow. Just wow. You, better than us?" asks Sierra returning some fire. This divides the group even further.

"You all have so much to say now," Cassius shoots back. "We all knew you felt this way about us, but now you have just aired out your true feelings."

"Speak for yourself," replies Sienna, putting her hands on her hips.

Rocky gets right in the middle of them. He is trying

to use his sheer mass to intimidate them into being quiet. "Stop with the smack talking."

"Says the guy who talks too much," exclaims Cassius, standing toe to toe with Rocky.

"I talk too much? You must be looking in a mirror, because you never stop talking," Rocky bellows right back in his face.

Things are really getting heated.

"Okay. Okay. We can continue this fight later, but right now, we need to figure out where we are," says Stone, trying to pull the group back together.

"Oh, blow it out your ear, Stone," says Magnus, as he turns and walks away.

"Forget them. Let's figure this out," says Rocky.

Rocky and Stone start to explore as much as they can in the dark.

There are multiple tunnels heading in all different directions along the outside walls of this chamber. It is dark, so they are trying to feel which direction to go. The walls are made of stone and stacked up higher than they can feel. They choose to head down one of the tunnels that is closest to where all the Selenixies are standing. They come across two lit torches where it would seem like a weird place for them to be. But this whole journey has been a little weird, so they don't question. They take it as a win. They grab the torches and check out the dirt floor, the stone walls, and ceiling.

"Hey, Stone, lets head back, so we can shed some light on the subject." Rocky chuckles, shaking the torch.

"Not funny, really not funny, but okay," adds Stone heading back to where they left the rest of the Selenixies.

"Where are we?" questions Rocky, looking so confused as the torch reveals the walls, floor, and ceiling surrounding their friends.

It is like nothing they have ever seen before.

"It's a dungeon, people. A dungeon," states Jett, shaking his head.

"What is a dungeon?" asks Leora.

"Of course, you all wouldn't know what a dungeon is," snarks Jett. "I should have expected that."

"Just tell us," states Leo.

"It's like an underground jail. It is not pleasant at all." Jett's annoyed by their naive little minds. "Life is not always sunshine and rainbows. Wow. Just wow."

It doesn't help that the dungeon is dark, so amazingly dark, even with the torches.

Stone and Rocky try their hardest to barrel through the wall. They try to use brute strength to push the walls down. They try to use their wings to flit out, but that too is a waste of energy since the ceiling is just as hard and sturdy. There is no use. After multiple attempts, the anger starts to heat up even more. Leo notices other unlit torches scattered about the floor. He thinks having more light may help diffuse the situation. He gathers them quickly and begins to frantically light them one by one for each Selenixie.

Jett just sits back, laughing at this overall chaos.

Behaviors are being displayed that have never come to light in some of the Selenixies.

Leora is very vocal about how this is all Aura's fault and how she always has to be in charge, and now they are in this situation all because of her.

"Aura, if you are our fearless leader, then lead us out of this place pronto," Leora demands.

Aura is completely taken back by her words. "Leora, this is not my fault. None of this is my fault. If you want to place blame, I will give you three guesses whose fault it is, and the first two don't count." Aura puts her hands on her hips and stomps her foot, fierce with attitude.

Her head turns straight in the direction of Acacia and Jett, now fully assuming these two are who Mystic Neoma was referring to of the Selenixies who could have caused the collapse.

"Really, you have to be kidding me. You blame everything on us," says Jett. "Do you even have an original thought? Where are your fancy Mystics now to help you?" Jett's words cut like a knife.

"Seriously you need to find new fall guys," says Acacia. "We have nothing to do with this."

"We all know you moved the stone that caused the collapse that sent us on this mission," yells Aura. She is completely frustrated and hurt, and those emotions are coming out through anger and harsh words.

Chantal steps in to try to smooth over the situation, but it is not helping at all. Even Chantal is angry. She jumps on the bandwagon.

"Listen you two. You have to accept blame where it is completely warranted. This is totally your fault." Chantal has no idea why they are blaming Acacia and Jett, but it seems like the best thing to do. Something has to be their fault, right?

"Do you even know what happened?" questions Acacia.

"No, but I don't have too. It must be you two," Chantal yells back.

They are interrupted by another fight breaking out.

Rocky's voice becomes very loud, like he is yelling at Stone. "No, dude, it's this way."

"No, bro, it's going to be this way," argues Stone.

"Yeah, let's let the meatheads figure this out, and we will be getting nowhere," adds Magnus.

Bianca doesn't say a word, but she is turning a crazy shade of blue from holding her breath.

"Guys, when she blows, we are all in trouble." Zira points to Bianca, who is up against the wall with her hands balled in tight fists.

"It's coming!" yells Cassius, as he begins to run away from Bianca, covering his ears.

At the top of her lungs Bianca lets out the most incredibly loud ear-piercing scream: "AHHHHHHH!!!!!!!!!"

They all stop in their tracks.

Chantal tries to step in and calm her.

Jett is having an overload of feelings; this is way too much to handle.

Acacia who would normally be at his side trying to help soothe him and reassure him that things will be okay, completely ignores him.

Jett is clearly in distress. He pushes his way past her to get away from all of the Bianca drama.

"Really, Jett, can you be any ruder?" says Acacia, flipping her hair. "I have had it with your nonsense."

"This is crazy," Aura says. "Even Acacia and Jett are at each other's throats."

"The two of them were always on each other's side,

even when they disagreed, and they were always a united front against the rest of us. This is beyond weird," says Stone, confused by what is happening.

At this point everyone has their plan for what they think everyone should be doing.

"Acacia, what is wrong with you? Why would you want to try to head north in the tunnel? We have no idea where it will lead to. We could be in even more trouble. Sometimes you don't think," says Jett, being downright mean to Acacia.

Acacia is not having any of his disgusting behavior. "Really? What is wrong with me? What is wrong with you? You are acting like such a child, and you will do the exact opposite of what I say just so that you can say this is your idea. And, by the way, your idea is completely wrong, not fully thought out, and downright selfish. But, that is your typical MO, so please back yourself up and go your own way," barks Acacia.

And then something completely bizarre starts to happen.

Chantal tries to intervene. "Guys, come on, don't go," but her voice is almost inaudible, starting to disappear. "What is happening?"

Slowly, one by one, their voices fade. It is a scary time for all of them.

"But," says Aura trying to speak.

"Help," mouths Acacia.

Leora opens her mouth but only a breath comes out. Tears stream down her face.

The silence is deafening.

Fear shows on all of their faces. This is one of the most terrible things that has ever happened to them.

Now that they have all lost their voices, they realize they will have to use their other senses to communicate with each other. They begin by using their eyes, watching each other, and trying to mouth words. And this begins to work, but it is hard to figure out who is going to be the one doing the talking. They are all still trying to talk at once.

Cassius tries using sign language, but not everyone can understand him, and they all get frustrated again.

Sienna finds a stick and begins writing in the dirt.

Leo is excited that this may finally work as they try to draw a plan on the floor of the dungeon. Even with no voices, they are still unable to come to a complete agreement on what their next steps should be.

So, they decide to just agree to disagree and split up.

Acacia and Jett are the first to leave. They are so furious with each other that the two of them storm off in opposite directions.

As they all individually navigate through the dark tunnels each with their own torch thanks to Leo, they start to regain some clarity and realize their part in the breakdown of their communications. They are able to acknowledge that they are at fault just as much as everyone else is. Some talk it out in their head and see all sides of the drama.

The tunnels are long, dark, and creepy. It gives them time to reflect, to think about how they could have perhaps made the situation better. The tunnels are getting brighter as they start to see the error in their way. Even the color of the walls seems to be getting lighter and brighter.

Each of them is excited to try to find each other and reunite so they can figure out how to return home. They all begin running down the tunnels to find each other.

It takes a little longer for Acacia and Jett.

They are walking slower, really trying to figure things out. They need to work through some additional trauma that they have pent-up inside of them. They feel unseen, unseen by each other and unseen by the rest of the Selenixies. They are judging themselves and others.

The farther Acacia and Jett get from each other their voices begin to return. They can whisper at first, but their voices get stronger and stronger as they realize how truly sorry they are for their cruel words. They have an epiphany. The two of them are soulmates and are always best together. Their voices get stronger and stronger.

Acacia and Jett need to put their personal egos aside and truly listen to each other. This is not a small feat for the two of them. They are both very headstrong and passionate about everything. As they travel farther away from each other, the more they miss the others and begin worrying about everyone's safety.

"Oh no," says Jett out loud to an empty tunnel. "Acacia needs me. What if something happens to her? I will never forgive myself." He starts to run to try to find her. "Acacia," he cries as he searches for her.

At the same time, down an opposite tunnel, Acacia is calling for Jett too.

The rest of the group emerges from the tunnels to a common area.

This area is much brighter than the rest of the dungeon, and it seems like the perfect area for them to reunite in, almost like a plan falling into place.

"Hmmm," hums Aura.

They all run to each other and begin embracing each other.

Chantal is crying, like always, but this time she has happy tears.

The apologies start to flow.

"Sorry," says Rocky.

"No worries," says Cassius. "I'm sorry too."

"Sorry," says Sienna.

"Sorry," adds Leo.

"I was wrong," adds Stone.

"It's okay," says Aura. "I am sorry too."

"I apologize," states Bianca.

"Sorry! All my fault," says Magnus.

"Sorry, I should have listened to you," sighs Zira.

"I'm so sorry my words were cruel," says Leora.

"Sorry for my part," says Stone.

Everyone wants to express their sincere regret for their personal behavior, but no one is taking turns. They start getting louder and louder.

They stop and look at each other and break out into hysterical laughter. They all fall to the floor rolling and giggling at their actions.

"Wait," says Sienna. "Where are Acacia and Jett?" She is very concerned.

They start getting nervous, and they start looking in different tunnels.

Aura stops dead in her tracks; she is startled by something. "Hey, Selenixies, come back together," she calls, loud enough for all of them to hear.

"But," says Chantal with a look of concern in her eyes.

"Trust me," says Aura, cutting her off. "It will be okay, I promise."

Chantal nods and gently takes Aura's hand.

A blue glittery mist appears.

Aura hears Mystic Neoma's voice telling her that everything is going as planned and to trust her. Aura blows a single kiss to the sky in acknowledgment. When she opens her hand, there is a blue Goldstone in it. She places it in her pocket.

Acacia and Jett emerge from the tunnel at full speed and slam into the group.

They all say in unison, "I speak my truth."

They feel their Selenite recharge again.

The blue glittery mist envelopes them swirling faster, and they all portal out of the dungeon.

Thirteen

TRIAL 6: SKY OF BRILLIANT LIGHTS

The blue light brings them to a strange land. The sky is completely tranquil, with purple and green dreamlike swirls dancing in the distance.

It is clear that the Selenixies feel safe here. A calm immediately washes over them. They are as comfortable and relaxed here as they are in Lumina. No trembling, no worry, they are experiencing a sense of peace. They could even feel their heartbeat slowing down. They are all completely exhausted seemingly from their journey, and they agree to find quiet spots to rest for a bit to relish in this feeling.

Most of the group sticks together. But Acacia and Jett, of course, need to do their own thing. So, they head in the opposite direction.

They aren't too far away, though, and Aura knows that they need time to reconnect. She is not worried at all. In fact, she is way too tired to worry. She finds a soft spot to lie down. As she is falling asleep, she and the others admire the light. It is like they are swirling in the perfect pattern to lull them into a restful slumber.

The dynamic duo of Jett and Acacia tries to find a place to rest far, far away from the group. Putting distance between them helps Jett's brain settle and shut off for a while. They nestled themselves high in a tree whose limbs look like they are dancing in the breeze. Soft moss draped around Jett and Acacia sways to the rhythm of the wind. They wanted to be as close to that beautiful sky as possible.

As Jett starts to whisk away into a deep slumber, Acacia becomes increasingly anxious. Her head moves back and forth and she squints as if she is looking hard to see something. The restlessness isn't enough to wake Jett. He is now snoring louder than Acacia's ever heard.

"JETT, JETT!" Acacia is screaming in a panic. Normally calm and cool, this is not like her at all. "Oh, Jett! Where is everyone? We need to return to the others right now."

Jett's eyes open as he realizes this isn't a nightmare, Acacia is actually in a full-on meltdown. He isn't used to seeing her like this, so he snaps up in a frenzy. Deep slumber broken, he is wide awake.

"WHAT IS GOING ON?" asks Jett, empathically picking up on her hysterics and feeling his own. This behavior is scaring him. It is so out of character for her.

"I had a vision. I saw what is going to happen, or maybe what has already happened to our friends," she cries, trying desperately to calm herself down so that he will be able to understand her and help.

"What are you talking about?" He is so confused by everything that she is saying.

"I wish I could make you see. It is terrible, simply terrible." Acacia's face is wet with tears.

She begins to flit around frantically, crying out and trying her hardest to tell Jett what she is seeing. She is pointing to the colored light and saying, "See? See? Right there!"

Jett can't see anything except the swirling colors. Jett grabs her by the hand, hoping to calm her down. He stops moving immediately and is in horror. By grabbing Acacia's hand, suddenly he is able to see her vision in the sky. Stunned not only at the vision but at this newfound power, his mouth drops open, and now he too is frantic.

"We must go! We have to leave now," Jett demands. "We need to find them. This can't be happening. They need our help. We will only be able to fight this if we are all together. We are stronger as one."

The two take off in hope that the others are close by.

These visions are new to Acacia, and this is the first one she has had. She is not sure how to control them. And she is so surprised that she is able to show it to Jett. She is trying to wrap her head around this.

Jett looks over at her and says, "When this is all done, you have to explain to me what happened today."

She replies, "As soon as I figure it out, you'll be the first to know."

The two come bursting through the bushes. It brings them right into the heart of the peaceful clearing. It is just about sunrise. Everyone must have finally fallen asleep after the night's adventures.

They split up, Acacia heads to Aura, and Jett heads to Stone.

"Oh, Acacia, whatever do you want?" Aura asks sleepily. "I am really too tired to deal with anything at the moment."

Even Aura has her grumpy moments. This was one of them. Exhausted and enjoying the peaceful slumber, she just doesn't want it to end.

But Acacia is visibly spiraling, waving her hands.

"Aura, stop and listen to me. Please!"

"Okay, let me just—" Aura gets cut off before finishing her sentence.

"No, Aura, please. This is urgent. I need to show you something," says Acacia, shaking with fear.

"Can this wait? I'm not fully awake yet. Just a few more winks of sleep?" asks Aura drowsily, trying so hard to just go back to sleep.

"NO, IT CAN'T! NOW! LET'S GO! We must get Stone and Jett," demands Acacia. She is not taking no for an answer. This is major, and they need to deal with this now.

"Okay. Okay," says Aura.

Jett wakes Stone and gets a similar reaction.

They all meet up in the center of the clearing.

"Okay, now that we are here and awake, what is going on?" asks Stone in a big yawn.

"Acacia, show them," barks Jett.

"Umm . . . Jett, it doesn't work that way," says Acacia, not sure how to activate this power.

"Well, why not?"

"I don't know how it really works," Acacia whispers under her breath.

"Okay," says Aura. "As you two figure it out, we are going to get some more rest," says Aura as she and Stone start to walk away.

Acacia grabs both of them, and boom.

The duo gasps.

They are horrified at what she is showing them.

It is all playing out in the sky, like Acacia is projecting her vision into the clouds.

The Selenixies are under full attack by shadowy figures. They can't fully see who or what is attacking them, but the shadows appear bulkier than the Selenixies. They are definitely more aggressive. Every one of the Selenixies is running in different directions, calling for each other, shaking and scared. They've never faced anything with even remote violence, so they are shocked and completely out of sorts.

The shadow figures are trying to catch them and trap them in cages made of stone and branches. The Selenixies flit all over trying to escape their traps. It is sheer chaos. Everyone is shrieking.

Aura begins to cry.

Stone is turning red with anger, an emotion he isn't generally familiar with, and it scares him. This vision is deeply disturbing.

"STOP," yells Stone. "Why are you bullying us and showing us how you can destroy us? Leave us alone!"

This is Stone's anxiety coming through. He's starting to spiral out of control thinking that Acacia and Jett are the shadows, when clearly Acacia is showing them this so they can come up with a plan as a united front. Stone just can't pull himself together enough to realize that they are all on the same side.

"This is not us," says Jett, very disappointed that this is something Stone would think they would do.

"I am so confused," says Aura, still very disturbed by what she just saw. "Is this a trick or some kind of prank?"

"I feel like this is happening right now but it's not," says Stone, trying to wrap his head around the vision.

"Acacia, do you know when this is going to happen?" questions Aura.

"I don't know," says Acacia. "Listen, on Lumina, Jett and I distanced ourselves from the rest of you. Not because we don't like you, but because you guys are kind of a lot. And Jett is so empathic, taking in all of the sunshine and rainbows became overwhelming for him. But we never wanted anything bad to happen. We never wanted anyone to get hurt. We just wanted space. All of this may be our fault, but it wasn't intentional. I promise you that."

Rocky, overhearing some of this heart-to-heart, but not knowing about the pending attack, comes up from behind Jett, and traps him in a bear hug, "Aww, bro, you do like us."

Everyone smiles for a second, but then the reality of what they just saw sets back in.

"How can we stop this attack?" asks Stone.

"I have no idea. We came right away, when we saw this, to warn you," says Acacia.

"How do you know this?" questions Stone.

"Have you had visions like this before?" asks Aura

knowing that this must be new based on Acacia's nervousness surrounding the power. "Mystic Neoma said we would have magic on this journey. First, we could flit. Then we could portal between worlds, and a few of the other Selenixies have mentioned heightened awareness, but this is clearly a magical power, Acacia. You were chosen to show us these visions."

"I don't know. This is the first one," says Acacia. "And it just happened. I don't know how to control this. Or if it will ever happen again."

"We can get back to the visions later, but we must find out who these creatures are and what they want from us," demands Stone. "Hey, Aura, do you think you can maybe contact the Mystics about this?"

"I don't know. The Mystics have always contacted me. I can totally try going to a quiet spot and talking to them out loud. Maybe they will hear me and come with some answers," says Aura. "Acacia, can you come with me? Maybe she can also explain your visions."

Acacia is secretly overjoyed that she is going to spend time with Aura. Aura needs Acacia's help here. She is trying to act aloof, but she is having a hard time containing herself.

"Jett, Rocky, and I are going to gather everyone else so that we can fill them in and start preparations. We don't want to be caught with our guard down," adds Stone.

"Yeah, let's go. It's gonna be a long day," Jett says with a nervous laugh.

The three of them head off to wake the others up.

Aura and Acacia walk to a clearing. They look up to the sky, with its dreamlike swirls swirling in an even more fantastical way almost like a celestial twister trying to make contact with Mystic Neoma, but not before Acacia's next vision.

"Aura, stop. I . . . OMG, Aura, I can't," whispers Acacia as she falls to the ground. She passes out cold.

"Acacia!" yells Aura as she shakes her. "You are scaring me, wake up."

Acacia opens her eyes slowly. Tears begin to roll.

"What is it? Did you have another vision? What is it? Tell me," insists Aura.

Acacia begins to talk slowly. "Give me your hand and see if this works again. I cannot describe in words what I just saw."

Aura takes her hand and begins to concentrate too. And there she is standing next to Acacia in her vision. A vision of all the Selenixies in the cages. The shadow figures from the earlier vision are surrounding the cages as light flickers from the Selenixies' core as if they are trying to steal the Selenixies' light from their very being. It is horrifying to see. The image flashes to a full moon. It's trying to tell them when.

"Wait," yells Aura. "Look! It's the flower moon."

Every month, the full moon is given a different name. Most are familiar with October's harvest moon. In May, it's called a flower moon. And the Selenixies, moon lovers that they are, know exactly when the flower moon is coming.

"We have to tell the others to prepare for the next full moon in three days," says Acacia.

"We will, but first we need to get to the bottom of

who these shadow figures are and what they want with us. We cannot lose our light," says Aura.

"Let's call for Mystic Neoma, maybe she will hear us and have some answers for us."

Aura and Acacia both begin calling for her separately.

"Mystic Neoma!" yells Aura.

"Mystic Neoma?" says Acacia shakily.

Nothing is happening. They turn toward each other, instinctively grabbing hands and looking directly into each other's eyes. Their bond is becoming stronger by the second. And together, in unison, they cry out, "Mystic NEEEEOOOOMMMMAAA!"

The sky brightens even more. The celestial twister touches down and engulfs the two surrounding them in twinkling starlight. What should be frightening to them, is actually bringing them comfort. They just know this is Mystic Neoma's way of answering their call for her. The twister begins to dissipate and through the stardust, they see the outline of a house.

"That must be her house," says Aura.

Now the outline begins to fill into a full three-dimensional home.

"Where did it come from?" questions Acacia.

"I'm sure Mystic Neoma will have some answers," says Aura confidently.

They knock on the door, and it slowly opens.

"Hello, I have been waiting for you," says the beautiful voice from inside.

"It's Aura, and this is my friend Acacia."

OMG! She just called me her friend, thinks Acacia,

glowing on the inside. She has been secretly dreaming of the day for as long as she can remember.

"Come in and join me," says Mystic Neoma.

"How did you know it was us?" asks Aura.

Acacia is freaking inside that Aura thinks of her as a friend and is having a hard time concentrating on the Mystic.

"I knew you would call on me when you really needed me, and I hope I have the answers you are looking for," says Mystic Neoma. "But just to warn you, there is only limited information that I am able to share with you."

"But you don't even know about the questions we have," says Aura.

"I am a seer, much like your friend. I see the future and what is going to happen," answers Mystic Neoma.

Acacia is focusing on Neoma calling her Aura's friend too and almost misses what Mystic Neoma says. Then it clicks.

"I am a seer? Since when?" asks Acacia.

"Since always, but as long as you lived on Lumina you didn't need your powers, so they were dormant. Until now. You will see that you all are very special and can do many different special things. You just have to be patient and let the gifts emerge on their own. And they will, at the right time. Aura, you are a seer also, but your gift has not emerged yet. Acacia, you needed to have your visions so that you and Jett would return to the others. So, your gift emerged now to help you see the danger that you all are in and how if you work as a team, you will be able to save all of the Selenixies," Mystic Neoma says so calmly.

"And when I touch others, they can see my visions too!" Acacia asks.

"Yes, that gift is necessary for you to let your guard down with all of the others," explains Mystic Neoma.

"I see," sighs Acacia. She knows what Mystic Neoma meant. She wanted to be close with the others but didn't know how until this power emerged.

"Okay, next question," interrupts Aura. "Who wants to hurt us?"

The Mystic gets quiet, and her face turns very pale. "It is pure evil. Demons, filled with hate in their hearts."

"Are these the ones who collapsed the realm?" asks Aura.

"They are one in the same," says Mystic Neoma.

Acacia looks surprised and relieved but also ashamed. All of her emotions are flooding her face.

"Acacia, why are you so surprised? This is a *good* thing, we know more of who and what it was so we can try to save Lumina," says Aura. "All this time we have had no idea. Mystic Neoma, why didn't you tell us about this before?"

"You needed to figure out how to work together on your own. And you have, you are doing it. I saw the way you two looked at each other when calling for me. I saw how Acacia and Jett immediately went back to the group to warn you. But I can't tell you more. You shouldn't even be here now," says Mystic Neoma.

"When I was here the first time, you told me it was an inside job. And now you are saying it's not? What is the truth? Why should I believe you? Did you lie to me?" Aura is hurt and her words show her feelings.

"I would never lie to you, Aura. I didn't know it was the demons. They were clouding my visions. All I was able to see were the two Selenixies messing with the power source. The demons were using their powers to blur themselves out and only allowing me to see those two," pleads Mystic Neoma.

"This is all so crazy," says Aura, feeling a little better but still overwhelmed.

"Okay, back to our bigger problem," says Acacia. "What are these demons called?"

"Helios," replies the Mystic.

"Helios? Who are they?" asks Acacia.

"They are the children of the sun. They want everything that is not theirs, taking everything by force, and leaving a trail of destruction in their wake. They enter a realm and strip away all the things that make that realm magical. It is always in the most drastic and devastating fashion, and we haven't been able to stop them," says Mystic Neoma, who is visibly distressed.

"We have to stop them," says Aura.

"Do you really think that we can stop them?" asks Acacia.

"The Helios think they can steal your light. Your light is what makes you the most special of creatures. They think that if they have your light that they will become the most wonderful things in the Universe. But what they don't understand is that no one can steal or put out your light. It comes from within. And no one can take that away from you. They feel that they don't possess this light. But they do. It's just that the hate in their hearts causes them to not be able to see that they are beautiful creatures too. The hate clouds their brains and causes them to be jealous of all things around them," spells out Mystic Neoma

The Mystic continues, "They think if they possess all the good things that others have then they will be good. They think that will make them happy. But this has just become an endless cycle of constant heartbreak. And no one has been able to break the cycle. And we have tried. They are fiery little creatures filled to the brim with hate. They put the blame on everyone else. It is everyone else's fault that they are not happy. They want to bring everyone down to their level of misery. I am so sorry I wasn't able to warn you sooner. I was waiting for you to return. I didn't see it until this morning, but the Selenixies were chosen to show the Helios their light," declares Mystic Neoma, with tears in her eyes.

"We will do it. We will free them of their constant misery. We will show them that we can all live together and lift each other up. We will show them that the light inside each and every one of them is beautiful and worth being celebrated. It will be us. The Selenixies can do this," exclaims Aura.

"Are you sure of this, Aura?" asks Acacia. "This is not going to be easy. You saw my vision."

"I did, but I think if we are prepared, maybe we can change the future."

"Is that possible?"

Mystic Neoma smiles. "Anything is possible. *If* you work together. Together you can overcome any obstacle that stands in front of you. I have no doubt that the

Selenixies will be the ones to put an end to the Helios rampage of rage."

"We can use each other's strengths and weaknesses to overcome this huge challenge," gushes Aura.

"We also have the advantage. We know what they are planning," says Acacia. "I think we need to get back and prepare for the next full moon in three days, and we know that is when they plan on attacking us."

Aura turns to the beautiful Mystic. "How can we ever thank you? Our land and friends would be lost if it wasn't for your help."

"You would have figured it out on your own. You Selenixies are amazing creatures, and I am so happy that you are beginning to trust your instincts and are evolving into the leaders in our Universe," says Mystic Neoma.

"I wouldn't go that far. Not yet anyway. But we've got this," says Aura. She is extremely confident in her words.

"I would," Mystic Neoma says. "You are a power force, and you Selenixies can accomplish anything together. Now go! Make us all proud."

The two turn their backs to her, but she is already gone.

Jett and Stone gather the others and are waiting for Aura and Acacia.

Jett is so relieved to see Acacia appear from the clearing. It takes everything he has to not run straight up to her and wrap her in a bear hug. But he has to act cool in front of the others. He has a reputation to protect.

Aura begins to spill everything to the group. She is talking at warp speed. The others look puzzled.

Acacia puts her hand on Aura's shoulder. "It's okay, Aura, slow down."

Aura feels a calm overwhelm her, and she is able to slow down and tell the others what is happening.

Acacia asks the others to touch her hands so she can show them what she has seen. She warns them that her vision will be scary. Her vision projects into the northern lights in the sky, for all of them to see. With every moment Acacia is learning more and more how to control her power and use it to the advantage of the Selenixies.

Each Selenixie has a different response. No one knows what to believe at first.

"I thought those two were the bad guys, moving the stones and all," says Rocky with a big chuckle, nodding toward Jett and Acacia.

"We are," says Jett half-jokingly. "Apparently, these dudes are worse than we are."

"I would say so," says Rocky.

"Are we not even going to address that it was their fault that we are not on Lumina and that they collapsed the realm by removing a gem? Are we going to just gloss over and joke about that whole thing and forget it because out of the goodness of their hearts they came back to help save us," adds Bianca.

"Well," points out Acacia, "we now know that the Helios were the ones who caused the realm to collapse. It takes a purely evil heart to cause the kind of collapse that we all experienced. We may have wanted to leave Lumina, but our hearts are not pure evil. I like to call us mischievous. We just wanted a little distance, not destruction."

"Call it whatever you want," says Chantal. "You are here, and you alerted us. So, let's get on to what we do now about these horrid little shadow creatures."

"Okay, okay," interrupts Stone. "We must make a plan that will help eliminate these Helios."

"Wait," says Aura. "I . . . I mean we," she says as she looks over at Acacia. "We don't want to eliminate them; we want to neutralize them and help them to see the error of their ways. Help them find the light they have within themselves."

"Are you for real?" asks Jett. "Aura, you can't be serious. Reform the crazy creatures that want to put us in cages and steal our light and powers. Some of us haven't even had a chance to be given powers yet, but no biggie. Let's just give them to the fire demons. Smart plan. I think it will definitely work."

"Umm. No," says Acacia, who looks over at Aura puzzled.

"So, we are going to fight? Defend ourselves?" asks Jett.

Rocky pumps a fist. "Let's do this."

"Okay," says Stone. "Let's make a battle plan."

"Wait, wait," says Aura. "We are not going to battle. We have seen how that turns out. When I first saw the vision, I was enraged. I wanted to attack and eliminate them all. I was just as mad as you are. I was full of rage and anger like I've never felt before. Then Mystic Neoma helped us release our negative energy and showed us what we can do that would be more positive."

"Yeah, but we have the upper hand. We know what's coming, so we will be prepared," says Jett.

"Exactly, we have seen what is going to happen. We have seen the destruction. We have seen the devastation. We have seen Selenixies in cages," says Aura, frustrated that she is not able to fully communicate to them how she feels.

"We need to prevent this," says Stone.

"And we will," says Aura. "But we need to use our brains, not our brawn."

"Face it. We don't have much brawn," snarks Acacia.

"Speak for yourself," says Rocky.

"Oh, yeah, Rocky, you are so tough," says Jett. They begin to roughhouse.

"Okay, okay. Back to the task at hand," says Aura, trying to redirect their nonsense. "They are powerful, and we need to be smart. We will prepare to take them on. But, instead of a hand-to-hand battle, let's use some wit."

"We know that they are trying to put us in cages to steal our magic. Let's sabotage their cages and add some of our own. We can set up traps and then draw them here. We are smarter than they are. They are filled with hate and vengeance, and that clouds their judgment," adds Acacia.

"That's not a terrible plan," Rocky says. "We could beat them though."

"Sure, Rocky, we can beat them," says Jett.

"Okay, so we go with Aura and Acacia's plan," says Stone. "Rocky, you, me, Cassius, and Leo will go gather what supplies we need."

"When is this all supposed to happen," asks Zira.

"In Acacia's vision, they attack at the next full moon," says Aura.

"Why does everything always mess with our full moons?" asks Sienna remembering the collapse happened during their full moon celebration.

"Focus, people. Focus," says Stone. "We might not be battling, but we still have a fight on our hands. We really must prepare. We only have three days. We need to create cages that they will not be able to burn out of."

"I never really thought of that," says Rocky.

"Maybe instead of cages, we should dig pits," suggests Magnus.

Jett is struggling, and Aura can tell, so she walks over to him.

"Jett why don't you go scout some good spots to dig the pits," suggests Aura.

He is so relieved to be able to just get away from them. All of their emotions are torturing him. It is like the weight of the world is on his shoulders, and he can't shut their emotions out. The grief is maddening.

"Holes. Perfect place for holes," Jett mumbles, as he flits aimlessly. Once he calms down, he is able to focus on the task at hand. "Ahh! There and there will be great. There too. Nice one there too."

Perfect, he takes some extra time to just stay away from the group and to not feel.

Meanwhile, the others are continuing with their preparations. They split up some plans and head off to get to work.

Acacia comes running when Aura screams her name.

Aura is stunned in place. Out of nowhere comes a vision of the most glorious Selenite crown. It is so vivid; she can almost reach out and touch it. And she tries to.

But before she can grasp the crown, she hears Mystic Neoma's voice in her head telling her that it's going to be tough, but they can do it.

Looking up to the sky, Aura blows a single kiss in acknowledgment. When she opens her hand, there is a Sunstone in it. She places it in her pocket.

They all say in unison, "I trust myself."

Their Selenite is super charged now.

The purple glittery mist envelops them and they are whisked away.

Fourteen

TRIAL 7: THE CORONATION

They land back on their beloved home of Lumina. Or really what is left of it. It's a mess. Some of the big evergreen trees are toppled over, the fields of tulips and wildflowers are wiped away, petals left in its wake on the ground. The once kelly green grass is now filled with divots and chunks of dirt are coming up by the roots.

"What are we doing here?" asks Zira, puzzled by what she is seeing.

"I guess this is where the battle is supposed to take place," wonders Leo, because he too is confused by their current location.

"We never really focused on where the battle was happening," says Stone, scratching his head.

Jett throws his hands up in frustration. "We were so worried about when."

"If there is to be a battle here like Acacia's visions showed us, we really need to prepare," Aura says, already trying to plan out how they can win the battle on Lumina.

The land is so devastated making that one obstacle already.

"It's so weird being back here," adds Sienna.

"I thought I would be so happy when we returned, but I am so nervous," adds Cassius trying to comfort Sienna.

"Don't worry. We've got this," Rocky says with his typical brand of confidence. Once again digging holes.

"We have the upper hand," says Magnus, agreeing with Rocky.

They are walking to find a place where they can begin preparing for the battle. Suddenly, all of them stop in their tracks. Their eyes need to adjust to what they are seeing.

"Is this for real? The entire Crystal Fortress is a pile of rubble," says Chantal with tears in her eyes.

There is a pile of crystals where the Fortress once stood. The Selenixies freeze for a moment, trembling and instinctively grabbing one another's hands. They need to feel even closer to one another as they stand amongst this wreckage.

"It is terrible," adds Leora, wiping her eyes.

"This is horrible. But we must focus on the task at hand if we have any chance of protecting what remains of our home," orders Aura.

"It is going to take all of us to do this," states Acacia, coming to Aura's side.

"We can do anything as long as we work together," says Stone as he walks through the group trying to bring up everyone's spirits. He high fives Rocky.

"We each have something to bring to the table. We

are each special and powerful in our own way, and in order to do this, we need everyone to band together." Stone puts his hand on Jett's shoulder, smiling at the group while giving this pep talk. "Now, let's get started preparing. We don't want to be caught off guard."

They all jump right in to prepare again.

Rocky, Magnus, and Cassius dig holes to trap the Helios in.

Sienna, Zira, Lenora, and the others collect supplies like water and berries. They figure water will come in handy for so many things and berries can be a good distraction if thrown and splattered during battle.

They all get to work on the jobs they are given. They know it is going to be tough, and they are not looking forward to the battle, at all, but they know it is necessary for them to complete their mission before it is too late. Returning to Lumina was a major surprise, and they all were really caught off guard. But what better place to fight for Lumina than on Lumina? It made everything so real for them. They know they are fighting for their homes and for each other.

Aura is deep in her preparations when a vision suddenly comes into view in her mind's eye. Mystic Neoma had mentioned that she was a seer also, but she didn't have time to give it a second thought. The vision seems so real.

In her vision, she is standing in the great hall of the Crystal Fortress. It was just as beautiful as ever and in perfect form. The walls are covered in twinkling gemstones, with druzy pockets of Amethyst and Lapis Lazuli and Citrine and Rose Quartz, the very crystals from which the Selenixies emerged.

The sunlight is bursting through, lighting the Fortress with a golden glow as Aura's sparkling green eyes shimmer, catching every sunbeam. She is standing tall yet humble, as the Selenite crown is being placed on her head by Mystic Neoma. She is surrounded by the other Mystics. The Selenixies are in a ring around them all.

It is all so beautiful and glorious. But how will this ever happen? Aura doesn't have time to make sense of it all, because she has a fight to prepare for. She shakes off the vision and gets back to work. She wishes this moment was under different circumstances where she could rejoice and revel in the thought that she is a seer. But she pushes those feelings away and tries to focus on protecting the Selenixies.

It is time.

The village is silent. All of the Selenixies are in place. They have everything set.

It is an absolutely perfect night. The weather is beautiful. There is not a cloud in the sky, and the stars are flickering like glitter against a black backdrop. It is sad that they aren't able to fully appreciate the glory of the night. Instead, they are dealing with a potentially life-or-death situation. The thought of being locked in wood and rock cages and having the core of their beings stripped from them is the worst possible thing to them. They are very scared, but they are trying to be brave.

Suddenly, it seems like the air is being sucked out of Lumina. The sky turns the deepest shade of black, as if the stars have been wiped out. The smell of burning reaches the noses of the Selenixies as the shadow creatures from Acacia's vision begin to swirl into view. As they land on Lumina, the shadow creatures become clearer.

The shadows start to fade, and the glow of fire starts to become visible. The figures are wrapped in orange and yellow flames and are radiating heat. Their quick motions create glow trails as they move. The Helios appear fully. They don't realize they've been seen by the Selenixies, so they begin to sneak into the village. They are trying to be very quiet.

The Selenixies are waiting for them, because they know every move the Helios are going to make. The waiting takes a lot of patience. Everyone is in place.

"They are hiding behind the rose bushes," whispers Acacia.

This angers Aura a bit because she loves those roses.

Aura whispers to Acacia, "Has your vision changed?"

"Not yet." Acacia tries very hard to have another vision, though she hasn't quite gotten a handle on controlling the visions yet.

"They stopped. Something is wrong."

Acacia gasps as she grabs Aura's hand, showing her a new vision.

This vision is a good one. But they are so real that sometimes they are completely overwhelming that Aura and Acacia are taken off guard.

Finally, some good news. Acacia's new vision is of the Selenixies being on top. They signal the others to put the plan to trap the Helios in the holes and not hurt anyone into motion. The Selenixies are about to turn the tables.

The Helios must sense the calm and begin to panic and scatter. The Selenixies are ready for them. Every move they make, the Helios get shut down. The Helios try to set things on fire. The Selenixies were right there with a barrel of water to put out the flames. They tried to rush forward, and the Selenixies were there throwing berries in full force blocking their way. The Helios bounce back from the berries, and the Selenixies throw water at them which startles and distracts the Helios again causing them more confusion.

New move, but then: boom, shut down.

Now it's time for the Selenixies to act. They take control and work on capturing the Helios and putting an end to the battle.

But the Helios will not give up. They are determined to destroy everything the Selenixies have built. The Helios change their tactics and try to trap the Selenixies by confusing them, taking off in different directions in random patterns.

The Selenixies do not know which way to run because nothing the Helios are doing really makes sense. The Helios run left, then quickly run right, then shift and run in a circle round and round, back and forth, up and down, and every fiery turn leaves a ball of smoke in the Selenixies' faces making it not only difficult to follow but difficult to breathe. This is the Helios tactic of confusion and chaos. So now everyone is running in different directions and there is a sound that's getting louder and louder.

The Helios are screaming. But not just normal screaming, it's ear-piercing screeches. Long, loud, high-pitched, and burning the Selenixies' ears. They've never heard sounds like this, the type that totally disorient you and make you plain mad. The Selenixies are covering their ears, but it doesn't do anything to block the sound. It only makes the Selenixies lose their balance as they are trying to run.

"Aura, I have a new vision, and this is not a good one!" Acacia screams over the noise.

Aura was distracted by Acacia's call to her. The Helios fiery hands grab Aura, wrapping their hands around her waist as they quickly toss her into a cage and take off. It happens so fast, and Aura is furious; she is fuming. How is she going to follow through with this plan if she is in a cage? Miraculously, she was not burned at all when these fire demons touched her, like she was immune to their fire. She could feel the heat but was left without a mark.

The Helios took off so fast because they can feel Aura is the calm to the storm, the water to their fire, her very presence overwhelms them. And because Aura is pure light and love, she cannot be burned by the Helios.

Acacia sees what happened to Aura and doesn't know what to do first. Focus on her vision? Help Aura escape the cage? She takes a minute to focus on the vision, hoping it will help. She sees the Helios with the Selenite crown. They place it in the center of a circle they made and begin to shrink away with their heads down. The vision is so bizarre. You would think that they would be happy that they now possessed the crown, but they are still fiery in this vision.

"NOOOO," she cries.

"What's happening?" Aura questions from the cage. She can totally see exactly what Acacia is seeing.

The Helios with the crown in the circle. Acacia is projecting her vision to Aura.

"NOOO!!" Aura yells.

She is the angriest she has ever been in her whole life. She is turning crazy shades of red. Her heart is racing, her temple is pulsing, her palms are sweating; she has never felt this helpless and as completely alone like she does in the cage.

Her friends are trying but nothing is working.

Aura looks up to the sky and screams. "I give up! I surrender!"

Every Selenixie who hears Aura yell this is shocked. How could she give up now?

Aura throws her hands up and beams of white light shoot from them.

"What the—" Aura blasts her way out of the cage.

You see, Aura wasn't surrendering to the Helios, she was surrendering to her higher power. She got so angry, but she knew she couldn't do this alone, this required help and it sure came right when she needed it most.

The Selenixies and the Helios are in complete awe of the pure beams coming through Aura's hands.

And she intuitively knows exactly what to do with this new power. She aims her hands at a Helio, and he is surrounded by this white light. It's encompassing him, pushing him away far from her. He is startled as he feels trapped in this bubble.

Stone yells to her, "Can you teach me to do that?"

"Sure, just not right now," she yells back.

The Helios on the ground begin to charge straight at the Selenixies.

Out of nowhere, Bianca puts her hand out to help and freezes them in their place. She can freeze things!

"How cool," says Bianca. She is very excited to have this power. "How awesome am I?" she says to Leo.

"I always knew you were awesome. Now, do it again," he says.

It is as the Mystics predicted. Their powers would come to them as they were needed. And since the shield has not been restored, their powers are going to help them save Lumina.

"Bianca can freeze time? Crazy! Kind of crazy, right?" says Leora, as she is trying to do what she can to help.

Acacia is distracted by the ever-changing future she is seeing. She can't focus on what is going on, and she is having a hard time distinguishing between reality and her visions. She feels completely useless.

Knowing how she is feeling, Aura tries to encourage her. "Acacia, keep watching. We need your visions to help us."

Jett, on the other hand, usually the tough guy, is crippled with all the swirling emotions. He is amazed at how terrible he feels right now. He thinks that the grief that he is feeling is bad and that carrying the grief of the Selenixies is bad. But this is an overload. The emotions are affecting him physically. He is paralyzed. He stands in the middle of this chaotic scene and can't move.

Stone is worried for Jett and can see that Jett can't handle this. Stone comes to his rescue and hurries Jett off to a quieter place, tucking him behind a pile of fallen evergreen trees knowing that their needles and branches may buff the sound of the battle before them.

Rocky is a powerhouse. He steps out in front of the Helios to give Stone the time he needs to help Jett. He is always willing to help out his fellow Selenixies. He grabs a bucket of berries and starts wailing them like paintballs at the Helios. He giggles a bit as they bust open and splatter red juice and seeds onto their faces. This keeps the Helios busy until Stone returns to the fight.

Stone rushes back to the group, joining Rocky.

"Hey, dude, I'm back," says Stone. "What's next?"

While Rocky thinks the berry blasting is funny, the Helios not so much. They start storming toward the duo angrier than ever. Stone and Rocky realize the Helios mean business, so they begin running, but the oak trees are making a quick escape difficult as they try to weave and bob through the forested area.

"Not sure, but these trees are in the way," answers Rocky.

Rocky looks at the tree that is blocking their path to safety.

He wishes the path was clear so they could just run through without dodging branches, sticks, and trees. He focuses on the next tree he sees for a millisecond wishing it wasn't there and BOOM. The entire row of trees glides in unison out of their way.

"Dude, what was that?" questions Stone.

"Don't know, but it was really cool. Let's see if I can move other stuff," Rocky yells with a smile while running in the path he just cleared.

Turns out, he can move anything he focuses on and wants to move. Rocky's power comes in handy. He and

Stone set off to protect some of the others. They always come to the rescue of some of the more scared Selenixies.

As they run, Rocky is clearing the path with ease. He is moving trees and houses all over, confusing the Helios, who had studied the remains of the quaint village and now are at a loss as things have been destroyed and are continuously changing.

Their powers are emerging at an alarming rate. Alarming for the Helios, not the Selenixies, because for them the powers are coming at the perfect time. This may all have to do with Aura surrendering. Each Selenixie is being filled with the purest of white light.

Stone is one step ahead of Rocky as they run to help the others. He sees Leo up ahead who is frozen with fear as he is being approached on each side by a Helio.

Stone thinks to himself, *If that was me the Helios would be running scared*. And then BOOM. A duplicate version of Stone stands where Leo was.

The Helios, shocked by this instant change of appearance seeing Stone instead of Leo, back off completely bewildered. As soon as the Helios back off, Leo returns to looking like Leo.

Stone realizes he can change the appearances of the Selenixies by projecting himself in their place.

Stone jumps in the air. Now they can really confuse the Helios considering water and berries have been their only defense which now they are quickly running out of.

The Helios went running to the other side of the village, where Cassius, Zira, Leora, and the others are scrambling trying to figure out how they can fight them off without the proper supplies.

A Helio runs straight for Cassius. He wishes the mailbox next to him was a bucket of water he could throw at the Helio. He looks at the mailbox for a millisecond and then BOOM. The mailbox turns to a bucket of water.

Cassius has the ability to turn anything he focuses on to the very water the Selenixies need to startle and distract the Helios. With this ability, he is able to help the Selenixies in the battle.

He looks at a bench, and BOOM, bucket of water to throw and more Helios scatter. He looks at a lamp post, and BOOM, another bucket of water, another startled Helio running. The water wards the Helios off for a moment, but this back-and-forth between Helios and Cassius is becoming like a boomerang.

Zira panics as the fighting gets too intense and wishes the Selenixies around her were anywhere else but in this crazy battle. She closes her eyes and sees a bubble. Something instinctually tells her to focus on this vision. She listens to this inner voice and focuses really hard. A giant force field bubble emerges and encompasses Zira, Leora, and Magnus.

"Holy moly!" Zira yells, completely amazed at what she is able to do. She loves that she can do this to help all her friends. She is trying to keep them all safe but doesn't know how long she can hold the force field bubble.

Leora is busy in the force field checking to see if any of the three are injured. It is in Leora's nature to care for her friends.

Magnus has a few cuts and scrapes on his arms and legs from trying to evade the Helios.

Leora looks at the wounds on Magnus, and for a millisecond wishes they were healed, and then BOOM, as if she had been doing this all her life, she lays her hands on them, and the injuries disappear. Her power revealed, Leora is a healer.

"What an amazing power," says Magnus, looking at her gratefully. "It's just what we all need."

Leora smiles at him warmly.

She gets to be the healer. She is amazingly grateful that she can help her friends.

Around the force field bubble, mayhem is ensuing still. Leo is doing whatever he can to stay out of the fiery hands of the Helios. He is trying to use the Helios tactic of running around chaotically against them. As he does, he ends up running straight into the path of a Helio who is charging at him. Just as the Helio is about to grab him, he wishes he was invisible for a millisecond. Leo blinks and then BOOM.

The Helio is left perplexed.

Leo is no longer there. He is, but they just can't see him.

Spinning, Leo returns to where the Helios are searching for him. He reappears and they gasp and start to follow him again.

But again, he blinks and is gone.

Leo gains the ability to make himself invisible, and the Helios are unable to detect his presence, so he is able to trick them. This is a great advantage for the Selenixies.

Magnus is loving his newfound power. He is running through the village deflecting anything that is thrown at him like a boomerang. To him this is so much fun.

Sienna is so disappointed that she hasn't yet received a

power. This doesn't seem fair. She is watching all the other Selenixies use their really cool powers. She is bummed. So, she hangs out by Zira so she can stay in the force field and stay safe.

Everything is happening so very fast that it is hard to follow all of the action. These Helios are crazy.

Finally, Chantal steps into the middle of the chaos. She has had it. She closes her eyes and takes a deep breath. And with every ounce of her being, all the way down from her toes, she yells, "STOP!"

Everyone stops in their tracks and freezes. Unbeknownst to Chantal, she is able to speak any language, so the Helios are suddenly able to understand her.

"ENOUGH," she yells. "Why are you all so angry?"

The Helios all look at each other, puzzled. No one has ever asked them that before. They don't really have an answer. They have just always been like this. This has always been the only way they know.

Chantel starts scolding them. "This is not acceptable behavior. You are not supposed to act like this. I will not tolerate these behaviors."

Everyone is stunned.

No one moves.

The Selenixies are so proud of her and also in awe of her ability to immediately calm the situation.

"Do you have something to say?" demands Chantal.

She stands there directly in front of these fiery terrors, not scared at all. This is so out of character for her. She is normally so soft-spoken. She never says an unkind word to anyone. And now she is so overwhelmed that she is disciplining these crazy creatures. She is so sad that something would want to hurt her beloved friends that she has been pushed to her limit.

"Well?" she shouts, her hands high in the air.

One of them, who seems to be the leaders of the Helios, steps out in front of her. He is wearing a different emblem on his chest, and when he raises his hand the rest of the Helios jump to attention.

"I'm sorry," he says shyly.

"You're sorry? You're sorry?" Chantal demands, her voice cracking. "You have left a wake of destruction everywhere you have been, and all you can say is that you're sorry. I think you need to come up with something more than that."

"We are *really* sorry," he adds.

"Why are you doing this?" questions Chantal shaking and trembling and softening in tone just a bit. She thinks that maybe if she knows why they are so angry that this will make a little more sense.

"No one has ever asked us why. Everyone is just so afraid of us all of the time, that we have constantly been on the defense, defending ourselves because . . ." His voice trails off and begins to soften to meet Chantal's tone. "In response to everyone being afraid of us, we have always just been this angry, and I don't actually know why."

"This needs to stop now. I want us all to live peacefully. And this is not peaceful. So, let's clean up and sit and talk. I do not like fighting. We wouldn't be afraid of you if you weren't angry and throwing fire and seemingly trying to destroy our beautiful home. This ends here."

The Selenixies don't fully understand what is going

on. They can't understand Chantal as she is speaking in Heliotite and not in the language of the Selenixies. They all look puzzled, so she then translates. No one ever in a million years thought that Chantal would be the one to put an end to this battle.

"Okay," says the Helio. "We will go and leave in peace, never to begin a battle again. We will leave you alone forever."

"Wait," says Chantal. "Not just us. You need to leave everyone in the Universe alone. You need to learn to be happy with what you have. You need to look inside and find your light and let it shine bright."

"We don't have a light. We are filled with darkness. We have been plagued with this for eternity. There is nothing good about us. It's not worth trying to fix. We are completely broken," says the Helio solemnly. He looks totally devastated.

The Helios begin to retreat. Defeated, they sulk away with their heads down.

"Wait," Aura stops them, "Chantal, can you help translate?"

"Absolutely! I want to see this whole situation fixed." She tells the Helios to wait a minute.

The Selenixies are beginning to understand that the Helios' anger comes from feeling misunderstood.

Aura continues via Chantal, "We are having our full moon celebration tonight. Would you like to join us?" Aura thinks that if she extends an olive branch of peace that this might help the Helios heal. Maybe they just need a friend.

Now everyone is confused.

"Did she just ask them to join us? Is Aura losing it?" wonders Stone. He knows where her heart is going, but he is still weary of these creatures.

Acacia steps up and whispers to her that they may need time to trust and to let them go.

The Helios retreat and leave in a portal, promising to never return again.

"I guess we can't fix everything," says Aura. She is feeling defeated, like she is letting the Universe down by not befriending the Helios.

"I guess not, but we will always continue to try," says Chantal with her continually optimistic attitude. "Besides, the Helios did seem to soften quite a bit. They knew we were trying to understand them, and if they find their own light, they may just remember the moment where their darkness began to soften right here on Lumina."

They all gather in a circle.

Aura looks at her friends that are surrounding her and says, "Together is my favorite place to be."

They all smile.

Aura hears Mystic Neoma's voice telling her that they did an amazing job. She looks up to the sky and blows a single kiss in acknowledgment. When she opens her hand, there is a Goldstone in it. She places it in her pocket.

They all say in unison, "I understand my divine purpose."

Their Selenite is fully charged.

Glitter in every color begins to swirl around them one by one.

First red glitter.
Then orange glitter.
Then yellow glitter.
Green glitter swirls next.
And teal glitter swirls.
Blue glitter.
Then the purple glitter swirls.
The seven bright hues swirl into a rainbow, whisking around them.

Fifteen

THE REJUVENATION

A swirl of rainbow glitter touches down right smack in the center of the rubble of the Crystal Fortress. The glitter dust spins and spins around the Selenixies blocking their view. They are not sure where they are exactly. Each time they were portaled they ended up in a different land. But when they returned to Lumina for the last trial, they figured they were staying on Lumina. So they are quite confused and are struggling to see where they have been portaled to now.

When the dust settles and things start to become a little clearer, the Selenixies realize they are still on Lumina. They are standing in the center of the Crystal Fortress, which is in ruins, with the most peculiar looks on their faces. They start to spread out and look around.

When they first returned to Lumina they only saw the Crystal Fortress from the outside and were only able to slightly see the true devastation of it. But now they are standing in the courtyard and have a better view. The Crystal Fortress is a pile of rubble inside and out. The Selenixies gaze upon it with sadness.

"How could this be?" asks Chantal as her eyes fill up with tears.

Bianca puts her head on Leora's shoulder and sighs.

"Okay, so now what?" asks Magnus, looking to Aura for guidance.

"This is a major letdown," adds Zira.

"I thought for sure that everything would be back to normal once the battle was over," says Leora sadly.

"Why did you think that?" asks Leo, looking around.

"I don't know, I guess I was just hoping ya know," Leona responds, shrugging.

She pats Bianca on her head to comfort her.

"So do you think we can rebuild it?" asks Leo. He is so hoping that the answer is going to be yes, but he fears it may be a no.

"Hold on. Are we just going to gloss over all that happened in the battle?" asks Cassius abruptly, changing the subject.

"No one wants to talk about the battle," adds Chantal.

"No, not the battle, the powers. Let's talk about the powers. We have magic. Does no one care about our magic?" asks Cassius.

Before they can continue the conversation. They are stunned by a bright light. The sky lights up. Swirling dust clouds of glitter sparkle in the light, spinning around and around like a funnel cloud until it reaches the ground.

The five beautiful Mystics step forward. Mystic Neoma leads the pack. They begin to walk toward the Selenixies.

The Selenixies are a little stunned and afraid at first. They are still in protection mode. They don't know what is happening to them and are still on guard. Rocky and Stone step out in front and gently guide the other Selenixies to step behind them. Their fear starts to fade as they feel the genuine love that surrounds them.

Aura jogs straight for Mystic Neoma. Her arms are extended for her.

They quickly embrace. Acacia follows Aura coming to hug Mystic Neoma. Aura's face is glowing as she turns back to her friends.

"I would like you all to meet the Mystics," says Aura. You can practically feel the excitement in her voice. "This is Mystic Neoma, she has been guiding us through our whole journey."

"I have been watching over all of you for many moons," says Mystic Neoma proudly.

"I don't know all your sisters' names." Aura looks a little embarrassed.

Mystic Neoma smiles. "I would like to introduce you to my sisters: Seraphina, Chantara, Brisa, and Lana."

"Hello," they say sweetly in unison.

The Selenixies respond not quite in unison, so it is more like, "Hey. Hi. What's up? Hello. Yeah." The unique greetings from each of them mix together into a mumble.

The Mystics all giggle.

"Welcome to Lumina," says Chantal. "We are so honored to have you here I wish I knew you were coming. I would have baked some sweet treats."

"No worries, sweet Chantal, we know that you all

have just arrived home," says Mystic Brisa, secretly wanting those treats.

Rocky jumps right in and heads straight to the point.

"So, we went through all of the obstacles so we could return home right. I have a quick question: Is everything ever gonna go back to normal? Or do we just deal? And, just FYI, that mess over there is not normal," Rocky says sarcastically.

"Yeah," adds Jett. "That's a hot mess. How do we fix it?"

Chantal wipes her tears. "Can it be fixed?" she asks softly.

The others are desperately waiting for an answer.

The Mystics can see their pain and feel how much the Crystal Fortress truly means to them. Without wasting another minute, Mystic Neoma begins to speak.

"Aura, do you have all the crystals you received after you completed your mission in each new land," Mystic Neoma asks.

"Yeah, they are all right here," says Aura as she empties her pockets into Mystic Neoma's hand.

"Did you notice that they are all the crystals that make up the ancient power grid?" adds Mystic Neoma.

"No. Do they?" Aura questions. "So, I have all the power needed to recreate the power grid?" This puzzles Aura.

"We know that the collapse wasn't your fault. But rebuilding it is your responsibility. You couldn't just put the crystals back for everything to be okay. You first needed to learn to live and love with each other. You needed to learn that you are always stronger together, even if you have disagreements. You needed to stop and think about how your actions affect the situation. And that you don't always have to agree with each other, but you should respect the choices and opinions of others. And you did," says Mystic Neoma.

"You all are truly inspiring," says Mystic Seraphina. "This journey could have really caused more division among you, but it didn't. It brought you all back together, which is what this journey intended it to do."

"And made you so much stronger," adds Mystic Lana.

"You earned the Crystal Fortress," states Mystic Brisa. "It is now truly yours."

"Really?" yells Sienna.

The excitement is contagious.

They cannot contain themselves. They start dancing around.

Mystic Neoma steps forward and calms them down. Her presence is very soothing, and the Selenixies instantly feel it.

"Come now, it is time," says Mystic Neoma.

They all follow her to the base of the Crystal Fortress.

"Are you ready?" Neoma asks Aura and Stone.

They nod.

A pathway lights up, showing them how to enter the rubble. They follow the light to what used to be the room that housed the ancient power grid.

Chantal starts to cry, seeing all of the destruction.

Bianca, too, tears up as she recalls fond memories of teaching yoga in the great hall.

Mystic Neoma tries to reassure them that everything

is going to be okay. They are all very reluctant to enter the rubble.

Aura stops in front of them and turns toward them. "We can do this. We can do this together. It is the only way we can do this. We are a team, an unstoppable force of nature. Our strength is in our bond. We are powerful. We are Selenixies!"

This gives them the strength to link arms and enter the ruins. But, even with Aura's encouraging speech, this task is not easy for them.

The trip into the collapsed Fortress is very emotional for all of them, which makes it doubly emotional for Jett. He is trying so hard to hold it together, but at any moment he could break, and no one would be able to control the flood of emotions that will be released from him.

"Steady, Jett," Stone urges gently. "You can do this. Just keep taking deep breaths."

Stone reaches for Jett's hand to help calm him down. It's amazing how close they've all become through these trials. It used to be only Acacia who knew when Jett needed a calming friend to help him through.

"Can we get this over with quickly? I am really trying here, Stone. But holy moly, this is intense," says Jett.

"You will be just fine," he replies.

And with that, Acacia steps in and shows Jett a quick glance of the future and how he makes it through without exploding, which is how he is feeling at the moment.

This is a relief for him. It puts his mind at ease.

They all walk together to reach the center hall. They are awestruck by the devastation. The crystals were splintered in every direction. Where beautiful arches once stood there were now impassable hallways. The ceiling collapsed blocking the passage to some of the most beautiful gem encrusted rooms. The druzy walls just seemed lackluster amongst the wreckage.

"How is this ever going to work?" questions Magnus.

"It's going to take a miracle," adds Cassius.

"Trust," the Mystics say in unison.

Mystic Neoma takes the crystals from Aura, and the sisters get to work.

In unison they chant a spell that has the ancient power grid reappear.

Let the grid come back to thee,
What was lost is now seen!

And out of nowhere the grid solidifies right before their very eyes. The only thing missing are the Crystals.

Neoma helps Aura lay the gems out on the floor in front of them.

"Okay, Aura. This was the first crystal you received," states Mystic Neoma.

"Yes, it was after the first trial," says Aura, picking the crystal up to look at it. "A Bloodstone. I am strong, steady and grounded."

"What was next?" asks Mystic Neoma, knowing what was next but allowing Aura the time to answer.

"Next, it was a Tiger's Eye, for the second trial. I feel creative and inspired."

"The third trial gem."

"We received a Sunstone." Aura recites the words. "I can accomplish incredible things."

Mystic Neoma smiles. "Oh, and my favorite of all the lands."

"The fourth trial was the Rose Quartz. I love and accept myself and others."

"Then would be the blue Goldstone from the fifth trail," adds Mystic Neoma.

"I speak my truth," replies Aura.

"Sixth."

"The sixth is Amber, I trust myself," Aura continues. "And last but not least the final piece to the puzzle, Moonstone from the seventh trial, I understand my divine purpose."

The Mystic directs Aura to place each Crystal in a specific spot.

A Sunstone here, Bloodstone there, the Moonstone goes up there, and the Goldstone down here, the Amber up to the left, and the Rose Quartz up to the right. Their voices were almost like a song.

Mystic Neoma helps Aura arrange the crystals until they are just right.

The sisters then sing.

"This is where you all come in," says Mystic Seraphina.

"Each of you needs to place one of your hands on a stone and the other in the hand of a Selenixie," says Mystic Brisa.

The Selenixies arrange themselves to cover all the Crystals, and then they join hands.

"Now," adds Mystic Neoma, "repeat after us."

We together in harmony are strong.
Grounded creative and inspired.

We trust, love, and accept ourselves and each other.
We speak our truth and see clearly,
understanding our life's purpose.
We can accomplish incredible things together.

"Again," the Mystics request.

The Selenixies start reciting the poem the Mystics taught them again.

And before their very eyes the sky turns a radical shade of purple with blue and hot pink streaks. The ground starts to rumble.

This would typically be terrifying, but the Selenixies are extremely calm and keep reciting the poem. And before they know it the Crystal Fortress rises from the rubble like a phoenix rising from the ashes.

The crystals begin to jut out in all directions. First to the left, then to the right. It is a sight to see, and if the Selenixies hadn't seen it for themselves, they wouldn't believe it was happening. Crumbled arch ways resuming their shape. Wall growing straight from the ground. Webs of crystals and gems encrusting the floors and ceilings. Bright vibrant colors splashing in different directions covering the walls and doorways. Prismatic shaped windows create rainbows across the main hall. Grandeur around every corner.

The light dances into the courtyard allowing the Selenixies to bathe in the sunbeams. The perfect spot for their full moon celebrations. The Crystal Fortress is back, and it is as glorious as ever.

They are in awe.

They admire the beauty of the Fortress.

It is back, but something seems to still be a little off.

No one can really put their finger on it. It is amazing, but not quite the same.

"Wow," says Sienna. "I forgot how amazing this place is."

"I know. I totally took it for granted," cries Zira.

"It is the most beautiful thing I have ever seen," adds Leora.

"I am so happy it's back," declares Leo.

"This is a wonderfully special day," Aura chimes in.

"I think this needs a big celebration," says Chantal. "And you know what tonight is, right?"

They all kind of chuckle.

"Hey, I am all in, if you make those amazing chocolate raspberry things I love," adds Jett, kind of smiling.

Giggling erupts from all the Selenixies.

They turn to walk out and get ready for the night's celebration.

"But wait," the Mystics call.

"There is one more thing," Mystic Neoma adds.

"It's not finished yet," says Mystic Lana.

"It does look different," says Acacia.

"There is one last thing before the Crystal Fortress is complete and back to its former glory," says Mystic Neoma.

They are all looking around trying to figure out what is different. There is a different vibe this time. Everyone becomes quiet, and the crystals start to glow a soft glow that makes them all smile.

"Something is weird?" says Zira.

"Weird?" questions Magnus.

"Yeah, but a good weird, ya know," adds Zira.

Mystic Seraphina begins to laugh. "I know why you feel weird or different because this time you all earned the Crystal Fortress together. It wasn't just given to you. You each have a little ownership over it. It makes it even more special."

The Selenixies smile at each other, really proud of themselves and their accomplishments.

"But that's not the last thing," Mystic Neoma says.

"Aura, it is time for you to step up and receive a very special gift," says Mystic Brisa.

"Me? A gift? No. I don't deserve anything special. We did this together. Anything that is given should be shared among all of us."

"This is exactly why you were chosen to receive this. Your selfless acts have stood out to us for a long time," adds Mystic Seraphina.

"Please step forward, Aura," requests Mystic Neoma.

With some reluctance and a little pushing from the others, Aura steps in the center of the circle of Mystics.

"This is long overdue," says Mystic Neoma.

The Mystics place a crown of Selenite on Aura's head as they hand her the Ancient Scrolls in a gilded package. The glow from the Crystal Fortress gets brighter and brighter. And fireworks and glitter fill the sky in the most amazing display of color.

The Selenixies cheer and jump up and down with glee.

They are home and happy.

It is the most perfect day. Even Acacia and Jett think so.

The full moon celebration is a little more solemn than

usual. The Crystal Fortress is decorated beautifully, like it always is. There are vibrant bunches of hydrangeas on the table.

The delectable treats are piled in towers. There is so much fluffy whipped cream. And the berries are so fresh and incredibly sweet. Chantal has outdone herself this time. She has held nothing back. She wants this to be the best full moon celebration. The Selenixies appreciate all of her hard work. They eat the treats, dance, sing and howl at the moon. They are loving spending time together and being one.

The evening seems to go on and on. No one wants it to end. But alas it is time to call it a night. They are all getting really tired. So, they head to their homes to sleep. But no one seems to be able to rest.

One by one they find themselves all gathering back in the center of the village. They just want to be together. They carry pillows and blankets, and all lie down together for the evening. They pile in really close as if they need to be touching each other to feel each other's light. They lie there staring up at the moon, basking in the moonlight. They stay like this all night. They don't want to leave each other. Even Jett finds comfort being in the middle of all of them.

The next night, things are a little back to normal.

Chantal is busy creating delicious treats.

Stone and Rocky have convinced Magnus to participate in some of their extreme sports.

Leo and Cassius head off to pick some berries for Chantal.

Bianca is doing yoga by the calla lilies.

Jett and Acacia are holed up in a cute little house just being together.

The village is starting to buzz again, which makes Aura feel better.

Sienna is still upset about not having an active power, so she chooses to take a little time for herself away from the others. She sneaks off to help her critter friends. As Sienna is talking to her little friends and asking them how they are, she realizes they are answering her.

This is new on Lumina. Creatures never spoke here like they did in the other worlds. And now, Sienna can speak to animals at home. For her, this is the best power ever, and she was upset that she wasn't going to have powers. Now, in her eyes, she has the best one.

Aura stands in the middle of the village with a smile on her face. *We are getting back to normal, and maybe things will be even better*, she thinks.

Then.

The ground begins to shake like they are having an earthquake. But an earthquake on Lumina? *That is impossible*, Aura thinks. She takes off running toward the scrolls.

"There must be something in here," she mumbles to herself as she flips through the pages.

The shaking stops.

Stone comes running to her side. "What was that?" asks Stone, visibly upset.

"I don't know, but you know I will find out," insists Aura.

As they emerge from the Crystal Fortress, Mystic Neoma is standing there holding the optic lens. "I am afraid I have some bad news," says Mystic Neoma.

"What now?" asks Aura, still tired and frustrated from the last journey.

"Humans," says Mystic Neoma.

"Humans?" says Stone. "What do they want with Lumina?"

"They want your Selenite," says Mystic Neoma with concern on her face.

"Here we go again," says Aura.

ABOUT THE AUTHOR

I could simmer down, but I like myself all feisty.

Kristie Ferrugiaro is a mother of three beautiful growing boys. She is also a wife, a teacher, a fundraiser, and an entrepreneur. She keeps her days packed and still finds time to fulfill her passion creating fantasy fiction. Kristie's creative side and wild imagination led her to create a fantasy world rooted in real, timeless, and powerful lessons.

To learn more about Kristie, connect with her by scanning the QR code below.

ACKNOWLEDGMENTS

To my husband Nick. Thank you for supporting me in all my craziness and embarking on this adventure with me. I could not have done this without your love and support.

To my boys Vincent, Nico, and Christian. Thank you for inspiring me. You have turned me into a certified chaos coordinator, and I wouldn't have it any other way. I love you more than words can ever say.

To my Mom and Dad. Thank you for giving me a wonderful childhood and helping me to foster my creativity.

To Jenn and Inspired Girl. Thank you for encouraging me and creating the space for me to let my imagination run wild. Without you I never would have realized that I love to write fantasy. You helped me create this new world. I am truly blessed to have you. And I look forward to the future of the Saga of the Selenixies.